Crossroads

Adapted by Jenny Markas
from the screenplay by Shonda Rhimes

SCHOLASTIC INC.

New York   Toronto   London   Auckland   Sydney
Mexico City   New Delhi   Hong Kong   Buenos Aires

ISBN 0-439-39744-8

Designed by Kay Petronio

12 11 10 9 8 7 6 5 4   2 3 4 5 6 7/0

Printed in the U.S.A.
First Scholastic printing, February 2002

prologue: Lucy

We were best friends. We were eight years old. And we knew *exactly* what we wanted out of life. So we put it in a box and we buried it.

Mimi, Kit, and I dug a hole out at Hemmings Field that soft, early summer midnight. We stood under a tree, gazing solemnly down at the shoe box on the ground. Mimi, all wild hair and energy to burn. Kit, her beautiful brown face all chubby. And me, Lucy. Blond hair, and those serious eyes I always see in pictures of myself as a kid.

The box was a work of art — or so we thought. Inside, we'd placed our most heartfelt wishes for the future. Outside, it was covered in stickers and glitter. We'd let our creativity run wild.

We wrapped it in plastic, so it wouldn't get ruined. Then

we carefully placed it in the hole and shoveled dirt over it until it was completely buried. We made a pact, then and there, to dig it up at midnight, the day of our high school graduation.

Now I don't even remember what the others wished for. All I know is, we thought we'd always be friends.

LUCy

I love to sing.

More than anything in the world, I love to sing.

I love to belt it out as loud as I can, then take it down to a hush. I love to hit the high notes, and I love to push out the low notes.

Am I any good? It's hard to judge. I guess I can carry a tune. But even if I couldn't, I'd still sing.

Because . . . I love to sing.

That's what I'm doing in my room. I have the boom box cranked as high as it goes, and I'm singing along.

Well, not just singing. I'm dancing, too. Throwing my-self all over the room, in my boxers and tank top. Shaking my head, shaking my hips, just *shakin'* it. Yeow! I am *hot*.

By the time the song ends, I'm standing on my bed,

arms spread wide, holding that last note with every ounce of breath in my lungs. I feel energized, awake, *alive*.

Then the door opens. But I don't hear it. I'm still holding on to that note — and that feeling.

"You're going to be late."

"Aahh!" I scream and fall off the bed. Then I jump up to switch off the boom box before the next song starts. "Pop!" I say.

He's standing there, holding my graduation robe over his arm. Frowning.

"I was just — I was —"

"Did you practice your speech?" he asks.

"I almost have it —" I begin.

"Lucy," he interrupts. "How's it going to look if the valedictorian messes up her speech?"

What can I say? He's right. I grab some papers from next to my computer and start to flip through them.

Pop hands me my gown. "Don't wrinkle your gown," he says. "I just ironed it."

Then he walks out the door and leaves me alone in my room. Alone with the evidence of everything I'd strived for over the past years: my old science projects, my ballet shoes, my first-prize ribbons, the award plaque that announces that I've won the Kingsford scholarship.

All that stuff means a lot to Pop. He's a mechanic. He

never finished high school, much less college. He couldn't be prouder of me.

I'm proud of him, too. And I want to make him happy. He deserves it. After all, how many mechanics do you know who could bring up a daughter on their own?

MImi

Do they even remember? Or am I the only one? It's impossible to know. I haven't spoken to Lucy or Kit in — years.

I walk down the hall on graduation day, one hand on my tummy. I touch my tummy a lot these days. It's like I'm saying, "Hello, baby. I love you."

Yeah, I'm pregnant. Me. Mimi. Who would have thought?

Inside, I feel like the same Mimi who helped to bury that box so many years ago. I was full of hopes and dreams then. I still am. Only now, some of them are for this little person growing inside me.

And some of them are my own.

I look down at the slip of paper in my hand. A notice in the newspaper. I cut it out days ago, and I've been carrying it around ever since. SLIDE RECORDS TO HOLD OPEN

AUDITIONS IN L.A., says the headline. I know the details by heart. I'm going. What do I have to lose? And who will miss me, anyway?

I walk by the jocks. They *own* one end of the hall, down by the stairs. They're all so loud, so confident. They barely glance at me.

The hip-hop dudes are slouching around at the other end of the hall. All baggy jeans, cornrows, and attitude. I guess you might think I belong with them, with my baggy jeans, tank top, and a bandanna barely containing my wild hair. But I don't. I don't belong with anybody.

Not like Lucy. She fits right in with her crowd. I try to catch her eye as I walk by, but she's deep in conversation with one of those clean-cut academic types she hangs out with. Probably talking about the latest theory of relativity or something.

And Kit? Forget about catching *her* eye. She sails down the hall, the only African-American girl in the popular group. They're all gorgeous, trendy, and — mean.

Kit's the *most* gorgeous, the *most* trendy — and the meanest.

She sees me. I know she does. But she looks away before I can even try a smile. Whispers something to her friend. And bursts into laughter.

Kit

"Girl?" I feel like saying every time I see Mimi. "How *could* you let that happen to you?" But I never say a thing. I never even let her catch me looking at her big-bellied self. I am so *over* all that "friends forever" stuff.

It's not like I don't have friends. I do. And they're the coolest, *hottest* chicks at school. We don't exactly *talk* much, unless it's about accessories — but hey, talk is over-rated.

That's what Dylan says.

Dylan's my fiancé.

Fiancé. I *love* saying that word. Just like I love looking down at this awesome ring he gave me.

Dylan's in college, out in California at UCLA. I miss him like crazy. Wish he could be here for graduation. Instead, I'll just have Mom and Dad. Dad'll be all choked up. Mom'll be jumping all over me to fix my hair, stand straighter, be prettier — be just like her. Now that I've lost all that baby fat, I have half a chance.

"Hey!"

That's Lucy, Little Miss Perfect Blond. Running right into me because she's in the middle of pulling on her graduation gown.

"Hel-lo!" I say. "Watch where you're going."

"You ran into me, Kit," she snaps back.

"Oh, you're too perfect to run into anybody?" I ask.

"What?"

Like she doesn't get it. "Straight A's, perfect attendance, teacher's pet. Perfect little Lucy."

She looks down at the ground. I get even more in her face. "So nice and good and sweet." Why does she bug me so much?

"At least I'm not a stuck up —" She mutters the last word so I can barely hear it. Ha! Little Miss Perfect isn't quite as perfect as she lets on.

LUCy

It's over. We're graduates! I can hardly believe it. Suddenly, everything's different.

And everything's the same.

Like Pop, frowning a little because I messed up that last sentence in my speech.

And Kit's mom. I watch as Kit poses for photos. Her dad's beaming as he shoots. Her mom's nagging: "Smooth your hair, Kit. More. Turn to the left, that's your best side. Chin up. Smile. Not like that. Like this." She strikes a model pose to demonstrate. Kit's mom is beautiful. I'd hate to have that to live up to.

Mimi is off by herself, as usual. I watch as Ms. Jenson, our choir teacher, approaches her.

"We missed you in choir this year," Ms. Jenson says to Mimi.

Mimi doesn't answer.

"So, what are your plans?" asks Ms. Jenson in this chatty voice. "For the future."

Mimi just looks down at her belly. Then she looks at Ms. Jenson.

Ms. Jenson blushes. "Mimi, you could take junior college courses," she says.

"I gotta go," says Mimi. She starts to back away.

"I wanted to meet your mother," says Ms. Jenson. She doesn't know when to quit.

"She . . . had to work," Mimi says. "She's very . . . busy."

It's a lie. I know about Mimi's mom. She hasn't shown up for a school event for years. And it's not because she's too busy. It's because — well, it's because she's usually too drunk.

I watch Mimi slip away. Then, before I can duck, Ms. Jenson approaches me and Pop. "Lucy," she says, beaming. "Your speech was wonderful."

Pop nods proudly. "Except for the part at the end where she messed up, she was real good," he agrees.

Thanks, Pop.

Ms. Jenson keeps beaming. "I hope you're going to continue studying music in college," she says.

I wish. In fact, I wish it more than anything. I want to tell Ms. Jenson how much I loved choir, how much I learned from her, how I hope to be a professional singer someday.

But Pop puts his arm around me. "Lucy wants to be a doctor," he tells Ms. Jenson. "A surgeon. Right, kiddo?"

Ms. Jenson looks surprised. "You do?" she asks. "You never told me that."

I just shrug. Pop's watching.

"Voice classes would make fun electives —" Ms. Jenson begins.

"No time for that," interrupts Pop. "We've gotta double major in chemistry and biology if we want to get into the best med school. Right, Luce?"

I'm exhausted — and bored — just thinking about it. "Yeah," I say.

"Oh," says Ms. Jenson. "Well, then." She looks totally bewildered.

Pop nods to her and gets into the car.

Ms. Jenson reaches out to hug me, and I cling to her for a second. "I'm all he's got, you know?" I whisper into her shoulder.

"Congratulations, Lucy," she says, letting me go.

I climb into the car next to Pop, and we drive off.

Back at home, I head straight to my room. I change into my grad night party dress, and then I just sit there in the middle of my bed, staring at my wall full of awards and feeling totally numb.

There's a knock at the door. I don't respond, but Pop

comes in anyway. He's carrying my diploma, which he's already framed, and a hammer. "We've gotta add this to the wall of fame," he says, pounding a nail into a clear space in the wall. He hangs up the diploma and stands back to take a look. It's a little crooked, so he steps back in to fix that. Then he nods. "There. That's good, isn't it?"

That's when I burst into tears.

"Honey!" Pop whirls around to stare at me. "What's wrong? Are you sick?"

"I'm fine," I manage to choke out, between sobs.

Pop digs into his pockets, but he comes up empty. He looks around.

"On the shelf," I tell him, still sobbing. He grabs a box of tissues and hands it to me. I take one and blow my nose.

Pop sits down next to me and rubs my back for a minute. He doesn't say anything. He just sits there.

"I worked really hard to be valedictorian," I say finally, clutching a soggy tissue. "Really hard."

"Of course you did." He's still rubbing my back.

I look at him. "It didn't feel like anything," I say. "I thought it would make me feel . . . I don't know. It didn't feel like anything."

He stares at me. "What are you talking about, it didn't feel like anything? It felt great!"

Sure, it felt great to *him*. But all I can say is this: "I never went to one football game."

He frowns. "You don't like football."

It's true. I hate the game. "But you're *supposed* to go," I say, trying to explain. "It's supposed to be fun. Like the parties everyone went to at Hemmings Field. I never went to any parties, never stayed out late, never just . . . hung out."

Pop nods. "Thank God. You have a good head on your shoulders. You stayed home and studied."

He doesn't understand. "Pop," I try again, "it's just . . . there are all these things I wanted to do. And I never did them. And I was getting my diploma and it was like . . . is this it? Sometimes, I just wish I could have . . . not missed out. You know?" I grab a fresh tissue and wipe my face.

Pop takes me by the shoulders. "Didn't we work hard for this?" he asks. "I mean, what's the point of your old man slaving away as a grease monkey if not to make sure you had the best? And now look at you. Valedictorian, Kingsford scholar, premed. You have everything."

Everything. He just doesn't get it.

I take a deep breath. I'm not crying anymore. "You're right," I tell him, smoothing my dress. "I guess it's just the pressure of graduation and all. You're right."

"Of course I'm right," he says, getting to his feet. He

heads for the door. Then he stops to take one last look at the diploma. "Looks good on the wall, doesn't it?"

"Yeah," I agree, without looking at it. "It does."

"Have fun at grad night," he says as he walks out the door.

MImi

Hemmings Lodge. I feel totally uncomfortable in this place. It's *so* not my style to be hanging out in some fancy inn. But hey, it's grad night. Gotta party, right?

I watch as cars pull up and drop people off. Everybody's dressed to the hilt. I look down at my thrift-store threads — too tight, like everything I wear these days — and sigh. Kit and her girlfriends arrive, looking like royalty. She pushes through the crowd as if she owns the place, not even seeing me.

Then I see Lucy, over by the stairs. She's by herself. I walk over.

"Not now, Mimi," she says, before I can say a word. "Okay?"

"Look," I tell her. "I just wanna know if you're coming."

She gives me a blank look. "What? Coming where?"

Do I really have to explain? "It's graduation night," I say. She still looks blank. "Hemmings Field."

Her mouth falls open. "Oh, God. I forgot."

No joke. "Are you coming or not?"

Just then, her date shows up. A preppy guy named Henry, or Stanley, or something.

"Ready?" he asks her.

Lucy nods. Turns to me. "I can't," she says. "I have plans." She grabs the guy's hand and pulls him away.

I watch her go. Strike one.

Later, in the bathroom, I corner Kit. She's staring at herself in the mirror, looking like she doesn't approve of what she sees. I lean against the sink, fold my arms. She glances over at me.

"Did you want something?" she asks, all irritated.

She can't scare me. "Are you coming at midnight, or what?"

"Excuse me?" she asks, giving me this stare.

"We made a pact, Kit."

"Are you serious?"

I just look at her.

"Look," she says. "You can do it without me. I have better things to do than dig up some old box." She pushes past me and leaves the bathroom before I can say another word.

I stare at the closing door, then kick the wall.

Strike two.

I do my best to enjoy the dance, but there's no pleasure in it. I have nobody to dance with, and everybody just stares at me when I try grooving a little by myself. Finally, the torture ends and we all stream out into the night.

Or at least I *thought* the torture had ended.

Kurt catches up to me as I'm leaving. Kurt. This hip-hop dude I used to go out with. I liked his tattoos — what can I say?

"How's the baby?" he asks, looking at my stomach.

"Drop dead," I answer.

He grabs my arm. "Look, is it my baby, or what?"

"I can't believe I ever went out with you," I tell him. "Let go of me."

"I'm trying to do the right thing here," he says in this sort of pleading voice.

"And what's the right thing, Kurt?" I ask him. "Ignoring me for the past five months? Letting your friends call me names? Spreading rumors about me?"

"I only repeated what I heard," he says. "About that guy. And you. In his car. At Christmas break."

Kurt's a lot taller than me and a lot bigger. But I pull my fist back and let it fly, right into his face. And he goes down hard.

Kit

After that scene in the bathroom with big-belly Mimi, I'm ready for some distraction. So I'm thrilled when I get a good look at the dude playing keyboards.

My friends and I are dancing in a circle in our rightful place: the middle of the floor. We *rule* this dance.

I can't stop looking at that dude. "What a hottie," I yell over the music, nodding toward him.

"That's Ben Kemble," says my friend Tiff.

"I heard he just got out of jail," adds Jenna. "He killed a guy."

"No way!" I can't believe what I'm hearing.

"Way. Everybody's talking about it."

We all stare at him. Killer or not, he's *so* cute. He just keeps playing. He doesn't have a clue that we're talking about him.

"Too bad," I say. "I'd love to get my hands on him."

"If anybody could," Jenna says, "it's you."

"Well, obviously," I answer. "But I'm off the market, re-member?"

"Please," says Tiff. "Dylan's at college. Who knows what *he's* up to?"

I flash the ring. "Talk to the ring," I say. "He's engaged to me." I see them exchange a look. "Whatever," I say, dis-gusted.

Later, I watch everyone leave, all paired up two by two. I look down at my ring, then back at the stage where the band is packing up. And I sigh.

LUCy

"It's ten paces from the *other* side." That's Kit. I watch, from behind a big tree, as she steps out to meet Mimi, who just paced off ten steps from the left side of a smaller tree.

"What are *you* doing here?" Mimi looks shocked when she spots Kit.

"Where's Lucy?" Kit asks, ignoring the question.

"She's not coming," says Mimi.

Kit shrugs. "You brought a flashlight. Good." She grabs it and heads in the opposite direction.

"Hey!" says Mimi.

Kit shines the flashlight on Mimi's face. "Were you crying?" she asks. Her voice sounds curious. Not sympathetic.

Mimi ignores the question. "Give me back the flashlight." She grabs it and heads back to her side of the tree.

"It's on *this* side," Kit insists.

"No, it's on this side." Mimi sounds positive.

"No, it's not." Kit is impatient now. "I remember exactly."

"I remember, too." Mimi isn't backing down. "It's on this side."

I can't stand it anymore. "You're both wrong. It's this tree."

Mimi shines the flashlight right in my eyes. The two of them take it in: me, standing next to a tree, a shovel in my hand. They stare for a second. Then they walk over to join me. Nobody says anything.

"Let's just get this over with, okay?" I hand the shovel over to Kit, then take ten careful steps away from the tree. Kit follows me and starts to dig.

"Whose idea was it to bury this thing out here in the middle of nowhere?" Kit asks.

"Yours," I remind her. "We used to play out here, remember?"

Suddenly, Kit stops digging and tosses the shovel aside. She gets down on her knees to brush away the rest of the dirt, and Mimi and I join her. Finally, Mimi reaches down and very carefully lifts the box out of the hole.

We all fall silent, staring at it. My heart does a little flip. Suddenly, I feel like I'm eight years old again.

"God," Kit says finally. "I don't even remember what we put in here."

"Me, either," Mimi admits. "Hold the flashlight." Kit shines it as Mimi rips the plastic from around the box and lifts off the lid.

"My Bridal Barbie!" cries Kit. She reaches into the box and pulls out a Barbie doll dressed in total bride gear: veil, long white gown, the whole deal. The dress is a little wrinkled, and Kit smooths it tenderly.

"I totally forgot about her," she says. "You guys. She was my wish! I wanted to marry Ken. We were going to have two kids and live in the Malibu dream house."

"Looks like you're getting your wish," I say. I can't keep the sarcasm out of my voice, but Kit doesn't seem to notice.

"I know," she says dreamily.

"Yeah," says Mimi. "If anybody's got a plastic, empty head, it's Dylan."

Kit's still gazing at the doll. "Shut up," she says absent-mindedly.

Mimi reaches into the box. "Lucy," she says, "I think this is yours." She hands me a delicate silver locket in the shape of a heart.

Automatically, I reach out to take it. Before I can stop to think, I open it. There's a picture inside. It's me, at three years old.

In the arms of my mom.

Kit and Mimi look over my shoulder. "What was your wish?" Mimi asks.

I stare down at the picture.

"I wished . . ." I pause. "I wanted to find my mom. See her again."

"Did you ever do it?" Kit asks. Her voice actually sounds kind of gentle.

I shake my head. "No. She lives in Arizona and my pop, he . . . doesn't think it's a good idea." I close the locket and put it around my neck. Mom left when I was three. It's ancient history now. Time to change the subject. I turn to Mimi. "What'd you wish for, Mimi?"

She reaches into the box one more time and pulls out a key chain with a tiny globe dangling from it.

"A key chain?" Kit asks.

"No," says Mimi. "The world." She closes her eyes. "I was getting out of this stupid town. I was gonna go all the way to California. I wanted to put my feet in the Pacific Ocean." She holds the globe gently in one hand and pats her stomach with the other. Sighs.

Kit snorts. "Well, there's a dream that's not coming true for a while."

Mimi looks up, her eyes flashing. "A lot you know," she says.

Lucy stares at me. "What's that supposed to mean?" she asks.

I dig into my pocket and pull out the crumpled piece of paper I've been carrying around. I toss it to Lucy. She unfolds it. Kit goes over to see what it is.

"Slide Records to hold open auditions in L.A.," Lucy reads out loud.

"So, I'm going," I say simply. "On Sunday."

I ignore their looks.

"*You* are going to L.A. to audition for a record company?" Kit asks in a let-me-get-this-straight tone.

"Yeah."

"You're pregnant," Lucy points out helpfully.

"So I'll wear something slimming," I snap back.

"And what?" Kit is sneering now. "You think you're gonna become, like, this big fat pregnant star?"

I grab the paper out of Mimi's hand. "I have a pretty good voice," I say. Which is shaking a bit at the moment.

"Whatever," says Kit.

"How are you going to get there?" Lucy wonders.

I try to sound casual. "I found a ride with this guy."

"What?" Lucy freaks. "No. Absolutely not. That's crazy. Mimi, you cannot go all the way to Los Angeles by yourself with some guy."

I can't let them see how much I want them to come. *Need* them to come. "So, come with me," I say, even more casual.

"What?" Lucy freaks some more. She and Kit look at each other, then back at me.

"Are you serious?" Kit asks.

"I'll sing lead," I tell her. "You guys can do backup. Kit, you could see Dylan! And Lucy — we could stop in Arizona. You could see your mom." I'm practically thinking out loud now. I'm brilliant!

Lucy bites her lip. She's actually considering it! Then she shakes her head. "Mimi, look. It's really not something that . . . I mean, I think . . .."

"It's stupid, is what it is," Kit says, tactful as ever.

"You know what?" I say. "Forget it. Forget I ever asked you."

The shoe box is lying by my feet, and I give it a kick.

Something slides out. A picture. Lucy bends to pick it up. "Oh, wow," she breathes.

We cluster together to see. There we are, the three of us, at age eight.

Holding hairbrushes like microphones.

Singing our hearts out.

"Look at us," says Kit.

"Yeah," I say.

"We were so young." Lucy is whispering.

After we stare for another moment, we break apart.

"Well," Kit says, "I have to go. I have to meet my friends."

"It's getting late," Lucy agrees.

"Yeah." What else is there to say? We start off in three different directions. Then I turn back. "Hey!" They stop and turn to look back at me. "I'm leaving from the trailer park Sunday at five A.M. If you guys want to come."

I turn and walk off before they can answer.

Back home, I walk through the flimsy front door of our trailer to find my mom sitting with her head on the table. An empty bottle of booze lies knocked over near her elbow. "Annie," I say. "Annie!"

She looks up. Stares at me with glassy eyes. She looks old. Old, and drunk. I sigh. "Annie," I say. "You promised." I hook my hands under her arms and help her up from

27

the table. Then I drag her to the bedroom, through the narrow hallway. It's not so hard. I've had lots of practice. "Did you even go to work today?" I ask her. She doesn't answer. "Do you wanna lose your job?" When we get to the bed, I flip her onto it. She curls up and I pull the blanket up to her chin. Then I stand there, looking down at her.

"I graduated today, Mama," I say quietly.

But she's already snoring.

Kit

I can't believe Mimi's serious. Like I could just pick up and go to Los Angeles, on some crazy whim! Get real, girl.

It's the day after graduation, and I'm working at my dad's hardware store, which is smack in the middle of Main Street. Where the action is. If there *was* any action in this town.

I'm at the counter. Behind me is a wall covered with gorgeous pictures of gorgeous me. Me in my cheerleading uniform. Me in a sparkly tiara, with my Homecoming Queen sash across my dress. Me in the arms of a stunningly beautiful dude: Dylan.

Daddy never took too many pictures of me when I was little and pudgy. But now he couldn't be prouder of his "two lovely ladies" — me and Mom.

Truth? That wall embarrasses me sometimes.

I try not to look at it. Today I'm fussing with the dress

on Bridal Barbie while I wait for customers. I yawn. Glance at the phone. Give in and dial Dylan's number.

Thirty seconds later, I'm in shock. "Dylan! What do you mean you're not coming home for the summer?"

I can't believe what I'm hearing.

A customer comes up to the counter. I put my hand over the phone's mouthpiece. "Dad!" I yell. "Customer!"

Then I put the phone to my ear again. "Dylan, you have to come home," I say, hating the pleading tone in my voice. "Because. I haven't seen you since Christmas. Don't you miss me?"

The stupid customer is still standing there, watching and listening. I ignore him. I hate what I'm hearing, and I hate the way it makes me feel.

I'm scared.

"Don't be mad," I say. "I wanted to spend some time with you. We have to plan the wedding and . . ."

I listen. And my heart sinks. "I'm sorry," I tell him. "I don't mean to bother you during finals. I'll let you go. Call me later, okay? I love —" But there's nothing but a dial tone. "Dylan?" I ask, as if he can still hear me.

I hang up.

The customer leans toward me. "I just wanted to know if you had any —"

I grab my Barbie. "Dad! CUSTOMER!" I yell. Then I walk out of the store.

LUCY

Mimi's out of her mind. Nuts. Crazy.

I'm not even *considering* her invitation. Me? Go out to L.A.? No way.

But somehow, I can't stop thinking about it. I'm in the garage with Pop, handing him tools while he works under the hood of somebody's old clunker. It's hard to pay attention to what he's saying.

"Dr. Johnson called today," he says. "Good news!"

I know what that means. Dad takes good care of Dr. Johnson's car, which means Dr. Johnson owes him a favor. "He got me the job at the hospital," I say flatly.

Pop doesn't even notice how not excited I am. "Those discounts I gave him finally paid off," he says proudly. "You get to start day after tomorrow!"

I'm hardly listening. I touch the locket around my neck. "Pop?" I blurt out. "Can I ask you a question?"

"Sure."

I pause. "About my mother?"

Pop comes out from under the hood and wipes his hands on a rag. "Okay," he says uncertainly.

I have to know. "Has she ever tried to see me?"

Pop's eyes mist up a little. "Honey . . . no, she hasn't."

I nod. "Because I was thinking. Maybe she's just afraid to visit. I mean —"

He doesn't let me finish. "Luce. We've talked about this. You don't have to feel guilty about your mother leaving."

"But —" It's not *guilt* I feel exactly.

"Because it didn't have anything to do with us," he says. "She's the one who walked out on a three-year-old. She's the one who should feel guilty. All right?"

Now I've upset him. "All right," I manage to say.

"That's my girl," he says, patting my shoulder. He goes back under the hood of the car.

Later — much later — I realize I can't possibly sleep. I'm lying in bed, holding the locket so I can see the picture inside.

I check the clock by my bed. Four A.M. I turn over and try one more time to sleep. It's no use.

I get up and creep into Pop's room. He's snoring away,

as always. Pop sleeps like a log. I tiptoe to his nightstand, open a drawer, and pull out an address book. I flip it open to the "C" page.

There it is, in his scrawly handwriting. My mom's address. "Caroline Louise Carson, 485 Hill Drive, Tucson, Arizona."

Pop snorts a little, and I look down at him. I feel so guilty. But I grab a pencil and paper and copy down the address, anyway. I stick it in my pocket. Then I pull out a folded note and prop it up on the nightstand.

He'll find it when he wakes up.

When I get to the trailer park, Mimi and Kit are already going at it. They are standing next to this ancient, beat-up convertible, with a pile of luggage at their feet. A guy with a guitar slung over his back is leaning into the trunk; I can't see his face.

The sun is just coming up. The breeze feels soft and warm. It's going to be a beautiful day.

But I'll be in another state by breakfast time.

If Kit and Mimi ever get things settled, that is.

"Nobody brings four suitcases on a road trip!" Mimi is saying. Her hands are on her hips and her belly juts out as she stares Kit down.

"Look," Kit retorts, "Dylan asked me to come to L.A. I

can't show up there looking skank. I have *standards*." She gives Mimi this look, and it's obvious what she's thinking: that Mimi has no standards at all.

Mimi gives up. "You just better hope it all fits," she says.

So far, I've been dragging my backpack along. Now I heave it onto my shoulder and step toward the car. That's when they see me. "I'm not going to any audition," I tell Mimi. I have to make that clear right away. "You can drop me in Arizona."

Mimi stares at me. "Fine."

"Fine," I return.

"Shotgun!" calls Kit, claiming the best seat.

"As if," says Mimi. "*I'm* sitting in the front seat." The two of them try to shove each other away from the front door.

Then the trunk slams.

And this guy is standing there.

Our eyes meet.

And there's, like, this electrical *thing* that passes between us. I can't describe it. But I feel it all over my body.

"You've gotta be Lucy," he says, his eyes never leaving mine.

"Yeah," I say. I look away. Suddenly, I feel shy. "So. You're taking us to L.A."

"Yeah." He grabs my bag and tosses it into the backseat. We stand there for a second, just looking at each other.

Then Mimi, who apparently won the fight for the front seat, starts honking the horn. "Move it, Ben!" she yells. "Let's get on the road already!"

Ben. His name is Ben.

We climb into the car. I get in next to Kit, in the backseat, and Ben slides behind the wheel. He's paying attention to starting the engine, adjusting his mirrors, whatever. I lean forward and poke Mimi. "Who's the guy?" I hiss.

"Oh, that's just Ben," she answers. "He's cool."

And we're off.

By the time we pass Pop's garage, we're already in roadtrip mode. I've pulled out my journal. Kit's reading *Bride's* magazine, using a felt-tip to circle dresses she likes. Ben's concentrating on the road. And Mimi's munching on Twizzlers while she reads an L.A. guidebook.

I watch as we pass the garage, turning my head to see it growing smaller and smaller as we drive away.

Kit

So, we're in Georgia or something. Mimi's looking out the window. Next to me, Lucy is scribbling in her journal. This dude Ben is at the wheel, driving fast but steady, rocking his head to the insane heavy metal that's blasting from the radio.

I can't stand it anymore. I meet Mimi's eyes and see that she can't, either. I slide forward, reach over the seat, start to touch the radio dial.

"What are you doing?" Ben demands.

"What is with this *music*?" I demand back.

"I like it," he says.

"Can we listen to something else for ten minutes?" I need a break. Desperately.

"No." His eyes are on the road. His face is stony.

"Come on, Ben," says Lucy, barely looking up from her journal.

"Be a nice guy," I urge.

"Please?" Lucy asks.

I see his eyes go to the rearview mirror. He looks at Lucy. She must be looking back at him. "Okay, okay," he says. "*Five* minutes."

Yes! I twist the dial until a pop station comes on. Aahh! *So* much better. Soon, Mimi and Lucy and I are singing along, bouncing around in our seats. Happy.

Ben's hands are clutching the steering wheel. He's gritting his teeth. He can't take it. Finally, he reaches out and grabs the dial. Metal comes thundering out.

"Ben!" I cry. Totally unfair.

"You said five minutes!" Lucy yells over the music.

He just shakes his head. "I can't listen to that. Forget it."

"Like this is any better," I say, sitting back, defeated.

He turns it up. Drives faster.

MImI

We stop at a gas station. Good thing. Being pregnant means I have to pee, like, constantly. I head for the bathroom, which is disgusting, while Ben pumps gas.

When I come back, I catch Kit flirting with this old guy who's walking by. He's staring so hard at her that he bumps right into his girlfriend. She gives Kit a look and smacks the guy on the back of the head. Kit just smiles.

Lucy gets out to go to the bathroom. I lean against the car, opening the bag of chips I just bought. It feels good to stand up for a few minutes.

"So," Ben asks as he puts the gas cap back on, "what's the deal with Lucy?"

How predictable. "Why? Do you like her?"

"No," he lies.

"I wouldn't try it, Ben," I advise. "She's not like us. She's *way* out of your league."

I watch as Lucy approaches the bathroom. She opens the door and I can practically *see* her gagging. It's so gross in there. Finally, she holds her nose and walks in. I smile at Ben and shrug.

Later, we cross the border into Alabama. When it gets dark, Ben pulls the car over and turns off the engine.

"Why are we stopping?" I ask.

"I'm tired," he says.

"So, let someone else drive." We have to keep moving.

"Nobody drives the cruiser but me," he says stubbornly.

There's no reasoning with him. "Whatever."

Lucy stretches and yawns. "So, where are we going to sleep?" she asks.

Ben gestures out the window. "There's a field right here," he says. "I've got sleeping bags and a tent in the trunk."

Kit sits straight up. "A field? You want me to sleep in a field? I saw a sign for a Hilton back there." She's freaking. And I admit I'm no happy camper, either.

Lucy hushes Kit.

"How much money do we have?" she asks.

We all just stare at one another.

LUCy

So we're sitting in this fluorescent-light waffle palace, counting our money.

"I can't believe you only brought forty dollars," Mimi says to Kit.

Kit shrugs, holds up her hands. "I have expenses. I had to have my homecoming dress custom-made. I *was* voted the queen, you know."

Mimi makes a face. "My dream came true," she says, sarcastically.

I'm ignoring their bickering, stacking the money on the table and counting to myself. "Did anybody make a plan?" I ask.

"What do you mean?" Mimi asks.

I take a deep breath, count to ten. "Like, how many miles you were going to drive in a day? Which towns you were going to stop in? How much gas money you'd need?"

It seems so obvious to me. You don't start off on a trip like this without a plan.

But they did. The three of them stare at the ceiling, avoiding my eyes.

"Okay," I say, sighing. I dig into my purse and pull out a calculator, a pen, a notebook. I start jotting down figures, adding and subtracting. "We have a total of four hundred eighty-six dollars," I murmur as I make calculations. "Which means we have" — I'm punching in numbers — ". . . for gas . . . and food . . . and . . . okay."

They all watch. "Is it enough?"

I can't lie. "It's going to be tough," I say, looking down at the paper.

How tough?

Try the Alabama Star Motel. Our room is beyond dingy. The furniture is shabby, the carpet is filthy, and the place is lit by a bare lightbulb in the middle of the ceiling.

"I am not sleeping here," Kit says as soon as I open the door.

"It's all we can afford," I tell her.

Kit dumps a bag on the floor and throws herself onto one of the beds.

It collapses.

Later on, Mimi and Kit are both asleep. Mimi's in one bed with Ben, I'm in the other with Kit. I peek over at

Ben and see that his eyes are open. "So," I whisper. "How come you're going to L.A.?"

"My uncle might have a job for me," he whispers back. "I'm going to check it out for a couple of weeks. If I like it, I might move there."

"What kind of job?" I want to know.

"He owns a couple of dry cleaners," Ben says. "I'd be a manager. The pay's good."

I can't quite picture Ben behind the counter at a dry cleaner's. "What about your band?" I ask. I've finally realized that he was the guy playing keyboards on grad night.

He gives his head a little shake. "I was just filling in the other night. I don't have a band. I don't really . . . join things, you know?" He looks at me, all intense. "Mimi didn't think you'd come on this trip," he says.

"Neither did I."

"Are you sorry you did?" he asks.

I look at him. I smile. "Not so far."

He smiles back. "Good night, Lucy," he says.

"Good night." I roll over, grinning to myself.

MiMi

When I wake up, Lucy's in the shower. I can't wait another minute to pee. I slip into the bathroom. She's
singing and it sounds so good that I stop for a second just
to listen. Then I can't help myself. I start to hum along.

She stops singing. "I'm *in* here," she says.

"I have to pee," I tell her.

I unzip. Then Kit opens the door and comes in.

"We're in here!" I say.

Lucy sticks her head out of the shower. "*I'm* in here."

"I just want to wash my face," Kit says. She starts
slathering herself with this gross mud stuff.

I flush.

"Hey!" yells Lucy from the shower. She turns off the
water, steps out, wraps a towel around herself. I'm wash-
ing my hands while Kit waits for her mud to dry. "I'm in
here," Lucy reports one more time. She squeezes her hair

dry, shoving me over so she can get some space at the mirror. We all start shoving. Then I reach out and dry my hands on the towel she's wearing. That's the last straw. "I'm in here!" she shouts.

"You're so touchy," I say.

She throws up her hands, surrenders her space, and sits on the edge of the tub.

"So, Mimi," says Kit, eyeing me in the mirror. "How do you know Ben?"

"Just from around," I say.

"He is so cute," she murmurs. "Don't you think he's cute?"

Lucy pretends to concentrate on drying her hair. "He's all right," she says finally. All three of us know what she *really* thinks.

"I can't believe he was in jail," Kit says casually.

"What?" Lucy freezes.

Now Kit's looking at Lucy in the mirror. "Yeah," she says. "He, like, killed a guy."

"Kit." I want her to stop. She's freaking Lucy out.

"What?" she asks.

"Excuse me," Lucy says. "He *killed* somebody?"

"He didn't kill anyone," I say soothingly. "I don't think."

"Mimi!" Lucy stares at me, all wild-eyed.

"He had a car!" I try to defend myself. "He was going to L.A. Don't be upset."

Lucy's shaking her head. "Don't be upset?" she asks. "I'm on a road trip with a killer, and you say don't be upset?"

Her voice is rising. Kit shushes her. "He'll hear you." She cracks the door, and we peek out. Ben is sitting on the bed, playing his guitar. He looks up and smiles at us. Lucy reaches over and pulls the door shut. Hard.

She turns to me. "Mimi. Do you even know him at all?"

"Well . . ." I figure I might as well tell the truth. "He used to hang out with some guys from the trailer park."

"Oh. My. God." Lucy sinks back onto the tub.

"So he may have killed somebody," I say, trying to sound rational and mature. "So what? He did his time. He paid his debt to society."

Lucy just puts her head in her hands.

I think she's upset.

Kit

Why did I do that? Don't ask. Sometimes I just make mischief. I don't know why.

Ben loads all our junk back into the car. Lucy heads out, and Mimi and I follow her. I see his face light up when he spots Lucy. "Hey, you all ready to go?" he asks.

"Yeah." That's all she says.

He doesn't catch her tone. "You wanna ride up front with me today?" he asks, smiling at her.

"I'm fine in the backseat."

"Oh." He seems puzzled.

"I'm gonna go check us out," she says, walking off toward the motel office. Ben watches her go. He's disappointed, I can tell. I decide to cheer him up. Keep myself busy. I hate being bored. "Can I sit in front?" I ask in my flirtiest voice.

"If you want." He barely looks at me.

"I want," I tell him with a special smile.

Now he looks at me. And he opens the car door. "Then it's yours," he says, ushering me in.

We drive and drive, through eentsy, dusty old towns and farmland scattered with little shacks. I'll be happy when we get through Alabama. In the backseat, Mimi's sleeping. I can't tell if Lucy is, but her eyes are closed.

"So," I ask Ben, "do you have a girlfriend?"

"Not right now," he answers, his eyes on the road. He doesn't seem to notice how I'm leaning toward him.

"No?" I ask, all shocked. "Really?"

"You're surprised?" he asks.

"Well, yeah," I say. "I mean . . . come *on*." I'm trying to let him know how cute I think he is.

But he still doesn't look at me. Instead, I see his eyes move to the rearview mirror, to check out Miss Lucy. "I haven't found the right girl," he says.

I'm not about to give up. I'm in mischief mode and it's too much fun. "And what's the right girl? I mean, am I your type?"

"You ask a lot of questions."

I move a little closer. "Do you think I'm attractive?"

Ben looks at me. "I definitely think you have something going on," he admits.

"So," I say, feeling triumphant, "I'm your type?"

He swallows. "Are you *trying* to be my type?"

I sit back. Flash my ring at him. "I'm engaged," I tell him.

"Then why are you flirting with me?"

"I'm not!" I say. "I mean, I didn't mean to." Now I'm all innocent.

"Of course you did," he says.

And that's about it. We don't talk much. He just drives. And drives. And drives.

After the sun goes down, we leave the highway and he pulls into a supermarket parking lot. Lucy hops out of the car. "I'll be right back," she says.

"I'll go with you." Ben looks hopeful.

But Lucy's barely glanced at him all day, and she doesn't look at him now. "No. That's okay." She walks away. Ben slumps in his seat.

"Lucy! Get me some chips!" Mimi yells out the window.

Lucy doesn't seem to hear, so Mimi jumps out to follow her.

I look over at Ben. He turns away. Forget him. I climb out of the car. "Wait for me!" I call.

The three of us sweep through the store. Lucy's in charge. (Not that we voted for her . . .) She stands by the register, watching as the clerk checks our stuff through. I grab the latest issue of *Martha Stewart Weddings* and start flipping through it while I wait. I think about Dylan.

Sure. At first it was just a convenient thing, going out with him. He was a football player, I was a cheerleader. But we've been together for four years now. He knew we were meant to be. That's why he proposed when he came home for Christmas.

Mimi shows up just as the cashier is finishing. She tosses five jumbo-sized bags of chips onto the conveyor belt.

Lucy speaks up. "Mimi, we can't afford all that."

"I'm eating for two, you know," Mimi says, patting her belly.

Lucy raises an eyebrow. "And the baby needs Cheetos?"

Mimi sighs. Slowly, she reaches out and takes all but one bag of chips back. As she's picking them up, she notices a big carton of milk. She holds it up. "Joke, right?"

"Milk is good for you." Lucy sounds like the school nurse.

"Gee, thanks," says Mimi, making a gagging face.

I'm still thinking about Dylan. "He's moving back home as soon as he graduates next spring," I say out loud.

"Who?" Lucy looks up at me.

"Dylan. I'm already planning the wedding."

Mimi shakes her head. "You're seriously going to marry that loser?"

"You don't even know him," I shoot back.

Mimi starts to say something. Then she looks away. She rubs her tummy.

"What's wrong?" asks Lucy, all concerned.

"Nothing," says Mimi. "It just kicked, is all."

Ew.

"Can I feel it?" Lucy asks. What a glutton for punishment.

"If you want," says Mimi. She guides Lucy's hand onto her belly.

"So. What about Kurt?" I ask Mimi.

"What about him?"

"He's the father, right?" I watch her closely.

She nods. "Right. Kurt's the father. But it wasn't working. I dumped him."

Lucy looks surprised. "You *dumped* him? You're going to raise a baby all by yourself?"

Mimi looks down. Looks away. Finally, she just pushes past us. "I'm gonna wait in the car with Ben," she says.

After she's gone, Lucy looks at me. "This is so typical of her," she says. "She hasn't even thought about her future. I mean, how is she going to get by with a baby?"

"Yeah, well," I say. "She did this to herself."

Lucy stares at me. "Kit!"

What did I say?

LUCy

That night, we stay in this quaint little motel that looks like baby log cabins. Everybody else passes out as soon as they hit the beds, but I can't sleep. I keep thinking about Pop and how worried he must be.

Finally, I slip out of bed and head for the pay phone I spotted near the motel office. I dial and push a bunch of quarters into the slot.

"Lucy?" Pop sounds frantic.

I can't speak for a second. Finally, I remember how. "Hi, Pop."

Pop is trying hard to control himself, I can tell. "Lucy," he says, and his voice is kind of shaky, "sneaking away in the middle of the night. I am very upset with you. Are you okay?"

I feel awful. "I'm sorry," I say. I know it's not enough.

I hear a slapping sound at the other end, and I know

he's smacking the counter near the kitchen phone. "Sorry?" he asks. Now he sounds mad. "Dr. Johnson went to a lot of trouble to get you that job. How do you think I felt, having to tell him you wouldn't be starting work today?"

Ouch. "I'll — I'll be back in a couple of weeks." I know it's lame, but it's all I can offer.

"No." Pop's voice is flat. "You'll come back now. You're usually so levelheaded! To do something like this . . . I'm surprised at you."

He's on a tear now. I just listen.

"What did we work so hard for if you're going to start slacking off now? You really disappoint me."

Suddenly, I can't stand to hear another word. Gently, I put the phone back on the hook.

When I go back into the room, there's just enough light for me to see that Ben is awake, watching me. "You okay?" he asks.

"I'm fine." I get into bed and turn my back to him.

The next morning, we drive through some beautiful Louisiana countryside as the sun comes up. I'm writing in my journal in the backseat. Next to me, Kit is sleeping. If only she knew the way she drools in her sleep!

Mimi's up front with Ben, but they're not talking. She's just staring out the window, quiet.

I look up to catch Ben watching me in the rearview mirror. "What do you write in there?" he asks.

"Stuff." My journal is private.

"Hey," says Ben, "are you mad at me or something?"

I stop writing for a minute. Glance at his eyes in the mirror. Glance away. "How could I be mad at you? I don't even know you."

Just then, there's this loud, clanking noise. Kit wakes up. We all look around. "What was that?" Kit asks.

"I don't know," Ben says, just as smoke starts to seep out from under the hood. The car starts to shake, and Ben pulls over. We all get out and watch the smoke. Ben reaches out to touch the hood, then jumps back. I could have told him not to touch it.

The car keeps smoking. Ben reaches into the front seat and pulls out his jacket. He wraps that around his hand and uses it to open the hood. He leans in to look while the three of us stand there, watching nervously.

"What's wrong with it?" Mimi asks.

Ben's voice is muffled. "I think it's the head gasket."

"You think?" Kit asks. "You mean you don't *know*?"

Mimi puts on a Ben voice. "Nobody drives the cruiser but me," she says. "And you don't know?"

"Hey, I know," Ben says defensively.

I sigh. "Give me your jacket," I say, walking toward him.

"What?"

"Your jacket. Give it to me." Mouth open, he hands it over. I wrap it around my hand and lean under the hood. I use the wrapped hand to poke around a little.

"Don't touch anything," Ben says nervously. "It's a very delicate car and you shouldn't play around with —"

I straighten up and let the hood drop down. It slams shut. "It's your radiator."

"It's the head gasket," he says stubbornly.

"Your radiator is cracked. What year is this car, a seventy-three? So, we're talking maybe three-fifty, plus labor." I hand him back his jacket. He stares at me. I just shrug. "My dad's a mechanic. I paid attention."

MImi

It's so hot. And I'm *starving*. Sure wish I had those chips Sergeant Lucy wouldn't let me buy. I just finished the one bag that did get by her.

We're sitting by the side of the road, waiting for Ben to come back. He headed off to find a garage that could fix the radiator, or the head gasket, or whatever it is. "I'm hungry," I say out loud, after my stomach rumbles one more time.

"How long does it take to find a tow truck?" Kit asks. She's putting up her hair, getting it off her neck.

Lucy looks up from her journal. "Ben's only been gone two hours," she says.

"I'm hungry," I repeat.

Kit whirls to face me. "Would you stop saying that? We heard you. You're hungry. So what?"

I don't answer, and finally she turns back to rummage

in her purse and pull out a mirror. She starts to fix her makeup. "We don't *have* three hundred and fifty dollars. Even if he gets a tow truck, we don't have enough money to get the car fixed. I'm gonna be stuck here in — where am I again?"

"Louisiana, I think," says Lucy.

"Stuck here in some dumb little town in Louisiana. I'm never gonna make it to L.A. to see Dylan. He's going to be so upset."

I can't help myself. I let out a snort.

"What?" Kit asks.

"Could you be more self-centered?" I can't believe her.

She doesn't say anything for a second. Then she faces me. "You're just jealous," she says.

I look at her. "What?"

"I'm not blind, you know," she says. "I know how girls like you looked at me in school. You would have given anything to trade places with me."

Lucy's ignoring this whole thing. Staring down at her journal. But I can't let that go by. I get to my feet. I want to laugh. I want to yell. "Girls like me?" I ask quietly instead.

Kit stands up, too. Faces me. "It's not my fault I'm popular," she says. "So just lay off."

"Girls like me?" I repeat.

Kit shrugs. "I didn't make the rules. I can't help it if everyone thinks you're trailer trash."

That's it. I give her a shove.

"Hey!" she says.

I shove her again.

Lucy finally looks up from that stupid journal. "Guys, don't —"

But it's too late. Kit shoves me back. "Knock it off."

"Take it back," I say, shoving her once more.

She shoves me. "Don't touch me again."

It's an invitation. I shove her. "Take it back."

Before I know what's happening, we're hitting each other. It's not the first fight I've been in, so I know what I'm doing. Kit's just flailing away, but some of her punches are landing. She grabs my hair, screaming. I smack her face, yelling.

Suddenly, Lucy's between us. "Stop it! Stop it!"

My fist, on its way to Kit, connects with Lucy's face.

Kit's hand, on its way to me, yanks Lucy's hair.

"Hey!" she yells louder. "KNOCK IT OFF!" She steps back and smacks both of us and shoves us apart.

I just stand there for a second, stunned. "Lucy —"

"Don't say a word," she says, her voice low. "I have had enough. I am so sick of the two of you complaining and fighting every second of the day. For once, would you just keep your mouths closed?"

"You don't have to be nasty," Kit says. Lucy takes a step toward her, and she shuts up.

But Lucy doesn't. She keeps raging. "I can't believe I did this. I can't believe I was actually stupid enough to get in a car — a *criminal's* car — with the two of you. I left my job. My father doesn't even want to talk to me. We opened some stupid box we buried ten years ago, and now I'm stuck here with you two! So just shut up. Shut up. SHUT UP!"

The three of us stare at one another.

"I don't know why I even asked the two of you to come on this trip," I say finally.

"We don't belong together," Lucy says, shaking her head in disgust.

"This was a mistake," Kit mumbles.

And then we all just stand there, silent. There's nothing left to say.

LUCy

I've had it.

I mean, I've really just had it.

Standing here in the middle of Louisiana, sweating my brains out, watching these two girls who *used* to be my friends fight like cats and dogs. . . .

I've had it.

I sit down on my suitcase and stare into space.

Finally, the tow truck comes and takes our car to a garage. We wait some more. Nobody's talking.

Then Ben comes over after consulting with the mechanic. "It's a cracked radiator," he says. (Big surprise.) "He can get it fixed by Monday."

Kit looks up, her eyes dull. "And how are we going to pay him?"

"I have an idea," says Mimi.

I don't want to hear it. I stand up and shoulder my

backpack. "I'm going to call my father and have him come get me," I say. It's time to get out of here. I mean, I don't know why I'm here in the first place! What was I thinking?

"I have an idea," Mimi says again.

Kit's staring at me. "You're leaving?"

"This trip is *so* over," I tell her.

Mimi's like a broken record. "I have an idea."

I whirl around to face her. "You know what?" I shout. "I'm sick of your ideas. I should have known you'd make a mess of this trip. Your whole life is one big screwup. I should know. I spent enough time fixing your mistakes when we were kids."

The look on Mimi's face after I say that is —

I can't look. I turn and head for the pay phone in the corner. Shove in some change. Start to dial.

Then Mimi grabs the phone out of my hand and hangs it up.

"Yeah," she says, her voice low and steady. "I made a lot of mistakes. And maybe I have made a mess of my life. But this trip? You wanted to come. Nobody made you. You wanna run home to Daddy? Fine. But don't you even try to blame it on me."

I grab the phone again and start to dial. "Forget you," I say.

"Forget *you*," she snarls.

We just look at each other for a moment.

Mimi crosses her arms. A look passes over her. Suddenly, I'm seeing the old Mimi, the eight-year-old Mimi.

"I haven't asked you for anything in a long time," she says, keeping her eyes on mine. Her voice is steady. "But I'm asking you to stay." Now her eyes flash a little. "Hang up the phone and *stay*."

There's something in her voice. I stand there for a second, holding the phone. Then I hang it up.

"I have an idea, you know," she says once more.

"Yeah, well," I tell her, "it better be good."

Kit

You are not going to *believe* Mimi's idea. The girl is out of her mind!

Picture this: We're in New Orleans. Home of steamboats, street musicians, tourists, Bourbon Street. Bourbon Street? That's where all the clubs are, where the tourists come to hear music.

And tonight?

They're coming to hear *us*.

I know. It's ridiculous.

Mimi found this place where anybody can take the stage. If the audience likes you, you can make a bunch of money. If not? Well, as Mimi points out, we have nothing to lose.

Nothing but our dignity, that is.

We're in the men's room at Club Bayou, getting ready. Ben's outside, making sure no guys come in. We're still

Kit, Mimi,
Lucy, and Ben
are following
their dreams on
a cross-country
road trip.

Mimi, Lucy, and Kit were best friends when they were kids, but things have changed. Until they dig up their childhood time capsule — and Mimi asks Kit and Lucy to join her for a singing audition in L.A.

Lucy's strict dad wants her to spend the summer getting ready for college, but she knows she has to follow her dream. She sneaks away from home to join her friends on their road trip.

Ben, a guy Mimi knows, comes too. Everything's going well...till the car breaks down and Kit and Mimi get in a big fight.

The girls and Ben need to make some quick cash to repair the car. Mimi's got a great idea — the girls will perform together at Club Bayou. But Mimi gets stage fright and it's up to Lucy to sing lead. They're a hit!

Performing together makes Kit, Mimi, and Lucy realize how much they still care about one another.

Sparks fly between Lucy and Ben when the group camps out in the desert.

California at last! And Ben and Lucy are closer than ever.

At the end of the road, Lucy's dream becomes reality. She and Mimi and Kit bury a new box, this time knowing they'll always be together.

not exactly speaking to one another, and the feeling in that room is tense, to say the least. I'm leaning toward the mirror, putting on some mascara, when Mimi speaks up.

"I have something to say."

We turn toward her.

"I know we're not . . . getting along and all. But tonight's important. So let's just be civil and get through this. Okay?"

I look at Lucy. She looks at me. We both nod. "Okay," we agree.

"Are we ready?" Mimi asks.

Lucy glances in the mirror, shrugs. "Yeah."

They head for the door.

I watch them go by. Lucy looks like she's going to a math club meeting. Mimi is looking skanky, her hair a wild mess and her belly sticking out.

"Hold it," I say.

They turn to face me.

"It's all the tips we can get, right?" I ask.

"So?" says Mimi.

"Don't either of you know *anything*?" I ask. I flip open my suitcase. I travel *prepared*. Inside is everything I need to get those girls looking *fine*.

Ben

I know. This is the girls' story. But I can't help jumping in here, because none of them can really tell this part right. I can. I was there, I saw it all.

Here's how it went down.

I'm standing at the keyboard onstage, surrounded by the house band. The place is packed with loud, happy tourists. Locals, too. Everybody loves Club Bayou. Big Jake, the owner of the club, steps up to the microphone, taps on it to get everyone's attention. The microphone squeals, and everybody shuts up.

"Tonight," Big Jake says, "we've got a new act. For all you tourists who don't know how we do things in my bar, we'll tell you the rules."

I see some waiters laughing.

"You get to decide if the group is worth your hard-earned free time," Big Jake continues. "So if you hate 'em —" He puts a hand to one ear, and the waiters shout it out.

"Tell 'em!" they yell.

"And if you love 'em," Big Jake goes on.

"Pay 'em!" The waiters shout.

The crowd goes wild.

Big Jake holds up a hand. "Be fair, be loud, and if you like 'em, be generous. You can show your appreciation by putting your cash in that basket located right over there." He points to a big wicker basket. "Now, these kids ain't got a name yet, but I got a look at 'em backstage and they're sweet young things. So here they are."

The crowd applauds as he walks offstage.

The lights come up.

And there they are! Mimi, Kit, and Lucy.

Wow.

Do they look different!

Well, Kit looks pretty much the same as always, maybe a little more glam. But Mimi? She's looking like one hot mama. Her top is tight, but somehow it hides her big belly. And her skirt? Shorter than short.

And Lucy. Well, what can I say? I never saw her looking like *that* before. Her hair is big, her tank top is very, very little, and her skirt looks like it's painted on.

Wow.

I notice that Mimi's looking kind of shocked. She's in front, ready to sing lead, and she stares out at the audience, her eyes wide.

But it's time to start. Lucy nods to me, and I play the intro to the song we've decided to do, "I Love Rock 'n' Roll," by Joan Jett. (It's a classic).

Mimi's supposed to come in after two bars, but she just stands there, frozen in place. I see Lucy and Kit behind her, looking at each other.

I start again, playing the first chords of the intro.

Mimi doesn't move.

From where I stand, I can hear Lucy whisper to her. "Mimi," she says. "Come on." Then she looks over at me, nods again. One more time, I play those chords.

I can practically see the sweat breaking out on Mimi's face.

And now the crowd is getting impatient. I hear rustling. Then I hear the first boo. And another. The boos are getting louder. "Get off the stage!" someone yells.

Big Jake steps onto the stage. He's going to pull them.

Kit panics. "Lucy," I hear her hiss. "Do something."

Lucy looks like she wants to run away. But instead, she steps forward and grabs Mimi's arm. She pulls her back. "You okay?" I hear her ask.

"I can't do it." Mimi is sobbing a little. "I'm sorry. I really thought I could. I'm sorry —"

"It's okay," Lucy tells her. "Stay back here with Kit." I see her bite her lip, take a few deep breaths. She glances out at the audience. Their boos are getting louder and louder.

Then she steps up to the mike.

She nods to me.

I play the intro again. And, with perfect timing, Lucy comes in.

She's a little nervous at first, her voice a little shaky. But after a few notes, the crowd quiets down. They can tell they're hearing something special. Lucy starts getting into the song, and I can see the nervousness slip away.

Now she's totally into it.

And she's good.

Really good.

By the middle of the song, Mimi and Kit are totally into it, too, singing backup and moving in perfect sync. Mimi doesn't look scared anymore. She looks happy and proud.

The audience is going wild. Lucy has them wrapped around her finger now. She's a natural. Money is flying into that wicker basket.

I play the last few bars, and the song ends. The crowd explodes into cheers.

* * *

Later, much later. The set is over. The wicker basket is overflowing. The DJ is spinning and everybody's dancing. Lucy and Kit are grooving in the middle of the crowd.

Mimi and I are at the bar. I'm counting the money, sorting it into piles. So far, all I can tell is that there's a lot. We'll have no problem paying that mechanic.

Big Jake leans over, nods toward Lucy. "She's welcome to sing in my bar anytime." Then he walks away.

I smooth out a few more bills and add them to the stack. Then I look over at Mimi. She's watching Lucy with this strange expression on her face. "You okay?" I ask.

"What? Yeah. Of course." She shakes her head. "I just — I just didn't know she could do that." She watches Lucy some more. "She's good, you know?"

"Yeah. I know." I stack three more ones on the huge pile I've made.

Mimi slips off her stool and goes to join the others on the dance floor. Lucy's ready for a break, I guess. She comes toward the bar. The two of them reach out and squeeze hands as they pass. Then Mimi joins Kit, who's busting moves that have everybody watching.

I guess their fight is over.

Lucy bops over to me, jumps onto a bar stool. "How much?" she asks, waving a hand at the cash.

I still don't have a total. But I know it's plenty. "Enough for the car and the trip," I tell her.

"We're rich!" She throws an arm around me.

I hug her back — but just for a second. Then she pulls away.

"Want to dance with us?" she asks.

I'm still reeling from that hug. I shake my head. "We should get going," I say. I'm worried that someone will figure out they're underage and shouldn't be in a bar in the first place.

"Oh, come on," Lucy says, smiling up at me with her head tilted. "Just a little while longer."

How can I say no? "Okay. Go ahead."

She dances off, happy as a little kid.

"Luce?" I call.

She turns to face me.

"You . . . you did okay up there," I say. It's not what I *mean* to say. But it'll have to do.

"I did?" She gives me a huge grin and dances off into the crowd.

This guy next to me is watching her closely. A frat-boy type. A little loaded. "She with you?" he asks, nudging me.

"What?"

"She your girl?"

My girl. Lucy. "No," I say finally.

I scoop up the money from the bar, leaving some for my soda. Frat Boy gives me a slap on the shoulder and slips off his stool, heading for the dance floor. I'm watching him go when Big Jake comes up to me.

"Y'all have some place to sleep tonight?" he asks.

I shake my head. "No."

He hands me a card. "A friend of mine runs this hotel. Tell him I said he owes me a favor. He'll give you a good discount."

I look down at the card. "Thanks," I say.

When I look back up, I see that Mimi has moved off the dance floor. She's sitting in a chair fanning herself. A guy has moved in on Kit, and they're dancing together. Frat Boy goes up to Lucy. She's dancing alone now, so when he starts dancing with her she smiles and nods.

It looks okay for a minute. They're just dancing together. But then the guy moves closer. Closer. He wraps his big arms around her and starts to move his hands all over her. I see Lucy trying to push him away, and I start to move toward them.

Frat Boy is still all wrapped around her by the time I get close. "Hey. Listen," I hear Lucy say.

Frat Boy tries to kiss her. She turns her face away. "Come on," he says, slurring his words. "One kiss."

Kit doesn't see, since she's dancing with her back toward Lucy. Mimi's over at a table, eating from a bowl of nuts.

"Stop it," says Lucy.

"What's the problem?" Frat Boy won't quit. He keeps his arms around her. Now she's struggling to get away.

"I said stop it!" she cries, hitting at him with her one free arm.

"Ow!" he says. "Come on. Be nice."

That's when I finally get close enough to put a hand on his arm. "Leave her alone," I tell the guy.

He barely looks at me. "Mind your own business." He pulls away and starts hugging Lucy even closer.

I look around for a moment to see if anybody's looking. Then, quick as I can, I elbow Frat Boy right in the nose. *Bang!*

He lets Lucy go, grabs his face. Blood is pouring out of his nose. "My nose!" he yells.

Everybody stops dancing. I see the guy's buddies over at the bar. They're getting up and moving toward us. "Let's go," I say. "Luce. Let's go."

She just stands there. I think she's in shock. I grab her wrist and pull her off the dance floor. We take off, running through the bar. "Kit!" I yell as we move out of there. "Mimi! Come on!"

LUCy

Ben's mad. No, he's *beyond* mad. I don't know what to do or what to say to him.

When we get to our hotel, Mimi and Kit start oohing and aahing over how fancy it is. They're right. It's shabby in sort of a classy way, but it's way better than any of the motels we've slept in so far.

"Is this living, or what?" Mimi says, taking it all in.

Ben doesn't speak. I watch him. He's making me nervous.

Kit races over to check out the little fridge in one corner, while Mimi heads into the bathroom. "I could swim in this bathtub!" she calls from inside.

I go over to Ben, who's leaning against a wall near the door. "Ben —" I start, not knowing what else I'll say.

He turns to face me, and I see his eyes flash. "I'm not mad at you," he says, and his voice is very low. "But I don't like having to do stuff like that. You understand?"

All I can do is nod.

He yanks open the door and stalks out.

Then Mimi pops out of the bathroom, all cheery. "Is anybody tired? I know it's three in the morning, but I'm completely wired."

"So, let's party," says Kit. She reaches over to the stereo (I told you this is a fancy place) and snaps it on. And the three of us start dancing.

I try hard to forget the look on Ben's face. But it's not easy.

We dance and sing along until we're nearly hysterical with laughter and exhaustion. At one point, Mimi's up on the coffee table, shakin' that big belly like you wouldn't believe. What a sight!

When we can't dance anymore, we settle in for a snack, rummaging through our stash and the hotel's fridge to lay out a huge spread. We even call room service when Mimi says she's craving ribs. And we start to talk.

Really talk.

"What's the best thing that ever happened to you?" I ask the two of them.

"Easy," says Kit. "Reaching my goal weight. Third year of fat camp, the summer before eighth grade."

Mimi puts down the ribs she's gnawing on. "That camp you went to every summer was a fat camp?"

Kit nods. "I loved it. For two months every summer,

my mama wasn't around to pick on me for being fat. Being fat is unacceptable to her."

"Wow." Mimi shakes her head, her eyes sympathetic.

"Okay," I say, "so what's the *worst* thing that ever happened to you?"

"That's even easier," Kit says. "Reaching my goal weight."

I'm confused. "But you just said —"

Kit smiles. "Turns out that being prettier than my mama is even more unacceptable," she says with a shrug.

Then she goes back to picking at her food. Mimi and I look at each other. Who knew?

After we eat, we dance some more. We take silly pictures with a disposable camera Kit bought. We put on mud masks and pose, sticking out our tongues. I haven't had so much fun — well, probably since I was eight and hanging around with these guys.

By sunrise, our room is a total disaster zone. Stuff is scattered all over the place: food, clothes, everything. Ben still hasn't come back, but I'm not thinking about that.

I'm thinking about my mom.

We're sitting on the balcony, which overlooks this outrageously beautiful garden. It's totally quiet, except for the trickling sound coming from a fountain down below.

"One morning," I say, out loud for the first time in my life, "I woke up and she was gone. Just . . . gone. Pop, he wouldn't say anything about it. I thought she was coming back. And then Pop told me she wasn't."

I look down at the fountain. Kit and Mimi don't say a word.

"They fought," I go on. "All the time. I think she just got fed up and took off without thinking. And then after a while, it was too late to come back. She'd waited too long." I take a long, shaky breath. "I know she wants to see me. She's just scared is all."

After a few moments, Mimi starts to talk. "Well, I live with my mama. But it's like she's not there most of the time. She's always . . . drinking."

"Is that why you never do?" Kit asks.

Mimi nods. "I did once, though," she admits. "Over Christmas. They had one of those parties, out at Hemmings Field?" She looks at us, and we nod. I've heard about those parties. "And this guy there was drinking this expensive, imported beer. I remember, it was in a blue bottle. I was mad at Kurt at the time, so when the guy offered me a beer, I had one. I had a few. And then he offered to drive me home."

She stops talking.

"Mimi?" I ask.

"It's no big deal," she says. "It just — happened. It happens to girls all the time."

I know what she's talking about. "Did you go to the police?" I ask.

She just looks at me. "I'm from the trailer park, Luce. I got drunk. I got in his car."

Kit's finally getting it. She gestures at Mimi's tummy. "So, it's not Kurt's baby?"

She doesn't really answer that. "I saw this ad in a magazine," she says instead. "So I called this lawyer in Atlanta. She sent me a bunch of stuff. Pictures and letters from people who want babies. Real nice couples with houses and big backyards." She looks down at her water glass. "I'm supposed to pick one."

Kit gets up and walks over to the railing. She hugs herself, as if she's cold. "The guy," she asks Mimi. "What was his name?"

Mimi looks up at her. She doesn't answer at first. Then she shakes her head. "I don't know," she says.

I reach over to squeeze Mimi's hand. "Why did we stop being friends?"

Mimi gives a little shrug. Sniffs. "I don't know. People drift apart."

After a second, Kit turns to face us. "Promise we won't drift apart again, okay?"

"Okay," says Mimi.

"Okay," I agree.

The three of us lean back to watch the sun come up.

mimi

We're all looking a little worse for wear as we watch our convertible sink down on the lift at the mechanic's shop. The guy backs it out for us, and Lucy counts the money into his hand.

Just then, Ben comes around the corner. He looks like he slept in his clothes. Or maybe like he didn't sleep at all. "Where've you been all night?" I ask him.

He doesn't answer. Just grabs his bag and rummages around until he finds a clean shirt. While Kit and I throw our luggage into the trunk of the car, he pulls off his dirty shirt.

Lucy comes up to him. "Thank you," she says. She sounds totally awkward. "For what you did, I mean. Last night. Thank you."

Ben just pulls the clean shirt on over his head. He takes the car keys from her hand and gets into the car.

*　*　*

Hours later we see a sign. "Welcome to Texas!" We've come a long way. Soon after the sign, Ben pulls over in a rest stop. Kit and Lucy and I get out to pee, and when we come back, chatting away, we realize that Ben is fast asleep on the backseat. Lucy holds up a finger, telling us to hush. We all look down at him. He looks kinda peaceful, lying there.

"Wake him up," says Kit impatiently.

Lucy frowns. "He's been driving all day."

I look around at the rest area. "We can't just stay here," I say. We'll never get to L.A. if we don't keep moving.

But Lucy shakes her head. "Maybe we should let him sleep."

That's when I notice that the car keys are hanging out of his front jeans pocket. "Fine," I say. "We'll let him sleep. Lucy, get his keys."

She turns to stare at me, surprised. "He told us we couldn't drive the car."

She's such a rule follower. "And why not?" I ask. "It's not like we're going to drive it over a cliff or anything."

Kit's convinced. "It *is* stupid to stay here."

I make up my mind. "I'll drive. Just get his keys," I tell Lucy.

She takes a step back. "Why do *I* have to get his keys?"

She just doesn't get it. "Because Kit and I voted. You lost.

Get the keys." I give her a little shove toward the car. She looks back at me, then tiptoes around to get a closer look at Ben. She takes a long, deep breath. She's going to do it!

Then she pauses. "This is stealing, you know."

I want to scream. But I keep my voice calm. "It's not stealing if he's in the car with us," I point out.

Lucy's still stalling. "No," she says. "It's kidnapping."

I don't answer. I just fold my arms and wait. Kit folds hers, too. Finally, Lucy leans forward. Very, very carefully, she slips her hand into Ben's front pocket.

Ben mumbles something and moves a little bit.

Lucy jumps back.

Ben sinks back into sleep. And I see Lucy look down at him with this soft expression on her face.

"Hurry up," I demand. She's losing focus.

One more time, she reaches out carefully and snags the keys. This time, Ben doesn't move. Lucy holds up the keys, grinning. We scramble to get into the car: me behind the wheel and the two of them next to me in the front seat. I stick the key in the ignition and start the car. It roars into life, sounding louder than ever. Eek! We all freeze. Kit leans over to check the backseat, then gives us the thumbs-up. Ben's still out like a light.

"It's okay," she says. "Go."

But I'm kind of paralyzed.

"Mimi?" asks Lucy.

"Give me a minute." I check all the buttons on the dashboard. Where are the headlights, the windshield wipers? I adjust the rearview mirror. Check the side mirrors. And then I sit there. I know Lucy and Kit are waiting, but I just can't —

"You failed Driver's Ed, didn't you?" asks Lucy.

"Maybe." I hate to admit it.

"Move over," she says.

I get out and go around to climb into the passenger side. Kit slides to the middle, and Lucy slides behind the wheel. She puts the car in gear and sails off without a moment's hesitation.

We drive for a long time in total silence. After a while, I can't take it anymore. I look back at Ben. He's still totally passed out. Then I nudge Kit. I nod at the dashboard. "Okay. Come on. Do it." How can we give up this chance?

Kit leans forward and fiddles with the radio. A second later, the car fills up with the sound of one of our favorite tunes, "Man, I Feel Like a Woman," by Shania Twain. Kit turns to smile at me, and I grin back. Lucy's smiling, too. We all start singing along at the top of our lungs. We're bouncing around, dancing in our seats, grooving to the sounds. We're happy.

"Hey."

I turn to see Ben sitting upright in the backseat. He

looks confused at first. Then he looks mad. I give him a huge smile. "Did you have a good nap?" I ask, still bouncing in my seat.

"Hey," he says again.

Now Kit turns around. "Don't be mad," she says. "You looked so sweet. We didn't want to wake you." She's sweet-talking him, batting her eyelashes.

"Stop the car."

Lucy keeps her eyes on the road, hands on the wheel. "It's against the law to park on the shoulder," she says primly.

"It's my car." Ben sounds as if he's trying to convince himself.

"We're almost at an exit," says Lucy, still driving as steady as ever.

Kit and I are watching the two of them, our heads moving back and forth like we're at a tennis match.

"STOP. THE. CAR."

Lucy pulls over, steps on the brakes until they screech. In a second, the car has come to a dead halt. The three of us are frozen in place, staring straight ahead. I don't dare look back at Ben.

Then we hear a door slam. Ben is outside of the car, walking up and down, his lips moving. He's talking to himself. We watch, terrified.

"Mimi, go talk to him." Kit nudges me with her elbow.

"*You* go talk to him," I answer.

"Nobody is going to talk to him," says Lucy.

"You're right," I say. "He's pretty mad. And he *has* killed before."

Lucy glares at me. "You said he *didn't* kill anyone."

I correct her. "I said I didn't *think* he killed anyone."

Ben just keeps pacing up and down beside the car. Up and down. Up and down.

Lucy sighs. She gets out of the car.

LUCy

We blew it. And I feel terrible. What we did was wrong, really wrong. I can't blame Ben for being mad. All I can do is hope he'll forgive us.

I walk around the car and wait for him to pace closer. "We're sorry," I say when he's a couple of feet away.

He stops in his tracks and gives me a look.

Then he starts ranting. "I've been stuck in a car full of girls for days. Do you know what it's like being surrounded by girls all the time?"

Well, yes. Actually, I do. I raise an eyebrow.

"Okay, yeah," he says. "Being a girl yourself. But I'm a guy. You know, a *guy*. And for days, I've been listening to pop music and girl talk and watching you all do your chick things. I'm a guy. I want to do *guy* things. And I haven't complained, because I know I'm outnumbered.

But my car!" He smacks his forehead. "It's, like, the only thing that wasn't taken over by girls. Okay?"

"Okay." What else is there to say? I hold out the keys.

He grabs them. "Okay."

He stomps back to the car. I follow him. He slides into the driver's seat, and I get in behind him. Kit and Mimi turn to look at me. I meet their eyes and shrug. Ben starts the car, and we drive off.

MImi

Texas is huge. *Gigantic.* It goes on and on and on. We've been driving through this brown landscape for what seems like months now, even though I know it's only days.

There is something beautiful about it, though, especially now, at sunset. There's no sign of civilization here, other than the highway. No buildings, no towns, no houses. Just miles and miles of wide-open spaces, spreading to the horizon.

Ben pulls over and stops. He gets out of the car without saying a word.

We get out, too.

"Why are we stopping?" I ask.

Ben just waves a hand. "Look."

We look. And we're speechless. It's one thing driving

through it, seeing it through the windows. It's another to be standing out in the middle of it. Suddenly, I feel very small. There's a hush; nobody speaks.

Finally, Lucy says softly, "It's like church."

"Yeah," Ben agrees.

"Like you have to whisper," Kit adds.

Something takes over me right then, and I can't help myself. I cup my hands around my mouth and yell, as loudly as I can. "HELLO!"

My voice is totally swallowed up by all that space.

At first, the others look horrified. But then they try it, too, screaming at the top of their lungs into that big, huge world.

We scream ourselves out. Then Ben turns back to the car. "We've gotta make time," he says. "The next motel is still an hour away."

Lucy puts out a hand to stop him. "Do you have enough sleeping bags for all of us?" she asks.

Ben's eyes light up. "Are you serious? You all really want to camp out?"

No way do I want to camp out. And I know Kit thinks the idea is insane. But Lucy looks at us, pleading. How can I resist? "Yeah," I say.

"Sounds like fun," Kit agrees, in a voice that says it sounds anything but.

*　*　*

Ben sets up the tent, far from the highway on a big, flat area near some bushes. I guess they're sagebrush, but how would I know? There are some cactuses and things, too. And rocks. And dirt.

Lucy's sitting by the campfire Ben made, writing in her journal while he adds twigs to keep the fire going.

I'll go out of my mind if I don't do something. Kit's dressed in her pj's, her hair in curlers like it is every night. We start to talk, and I'm not sure how it happens, but suddenly I'm showing her some of the tips I learned during all those years growing up in the trailer park.

Fighting tips.

"You have to keep your thumb on the outside." I show her my fist. "Like this." It's important to do that, or else your thumb can break when you hit somebody. Danny Towsley taught me that.

Kit makes a fist.

It's lame. But she'll learn.

"Right," I say. "Now, the trick is, don't let him know you're going to hit him. Maybe look away first. Or let your lip tremble, like you're about to cry. You know, something girly. Then when he least expects it, you throw your whole body into it and you punch him right here." I point to a spot just under my chin. Kit nods. She punches at the air in this experimental way. Way too timid. She's hopeless. But we'll keep working on it.

Lucy sees us and calls over. "Mimi, what are you doing to her?"

"I'm teaching her how to fight," I explain. "She should know how to throw a decent punch." Kit puts down her fist and we wander back over to the campfire.

"I'm going to bed," Kit says. She grabs her little cosmetics bag and crawls into the tent.

"And I'm going to the ladies' room." As usual, I have to pee. "Where is it again?"

"Third bush after the rock," Lucy tells me.

I pick up a flashlight and head into the darkness. I'm scared, but what can you do? "There better not be any wild animals out there."

LUCy

Mimi's stumbling through the bushes, and Kit's in the tent. It's so quiet I can hear my heart beating. The only real sounds come from the fire, crackling and snapping. I write a few more lines in my journal.

"What are you always writing in there?" Ben's voice makes me jump a little, coming out of the darkness.

"Nothing." I close the book. "Just stuff. Poems, mostly."

"Can I hear one?"

He can't be serious. "You don't want to hear one. Trust me."

"No, I really do." His voice is soft. He means it.

I *never* let anybody read my journal. It's, like, my heart. But there's something about Ben. . . . "Okay." I open the book. "One. But you can't laugh." I flip through the pages.

Find something I hope won't embarrass me to death. Clear my throat. And read it out loud.

I finish and close the book.

Ben's completely quiet.

"I told you you didn't want to hear it," I say. I want to die, I'm so humiliated.

"No," he says. "I liked it."

"Really?"

"Yeah."

Somehow, I can tell he really means it.

"So," he goes on, "how come you're not coming to Los Angeles?"

"This audition . . ." How can I explain it? "It's not really my thing."

"But Luce, you have a great voice."

"It's just not . . . practical," I tell him. "I want to see my mom, and I left this job back home, and my father —" I think of Pop, and my voice breaks.

"What about him?" Ben's voice is gentle.

"He's got a lot of plans for me, you know?"

Ben doesn't really understand. "Well, that's good. Isn't it? I mean, at least he cares."

"Yeah, but . . ." I heave a huge sigh and poke at the fire with a stick. "You do what you have to do, right?"

Ben shakes his head. "I don't think so."

"That's because you've never met my father." How can

he know what it's like to have someone's hopes and dreams riding on your every move? I look away. Ben's quiet and so am I. Then he leans over, closer.

"You have ash on your face," he says.

"Where?" I rub my face with my hand.

"I'll get it," he says, leaning even closer. He reaches out and gently brushes off my face. Then he just looks at me. He doesn't move. I don't move, either. We're very, very close. And very quiet.

Then Mimi bursts out from behind the tent, screaming.

MIMI

I haven't screamed like that since the last time I rode on a roller coaster, but I can't stop myself. I run toward the campfire, swatting myself on the butt. I notice Ben and Lucy kind of jumping apart; what was going on *there*?

Kit dashes out of the tent. "What happened?"

"Something bit me!"

"It did not," Ben says. "Let me see."

"NO!" I'm not about to show him.

"I'll look," says Lucy.

"Turn around," I tell Ben. He rolls his eyes, but he turns his back. I roll down my pants, just enough for Lucy to see. She and Kit examine me closely. "Is it a snakebite?" I ask, my voice all trembly. "It's a snakebite, isn't it?"

"That is a mosquito bite," Lucy says. I think she's trying not to laugh.

Ben turns around, and I pull up my pants in a big hurry. "Mimi," he begins.

"Well, it *could* have been a snake," I insist.

Kit just shakes her head. "We are out of here at the crack of dawn. Nothing is going to bite *my* butt."

She and I head for the tent. I'm still a little shaky.

Outside, I hear Ben and Lucy talking low. "We should put out the fire and turn in," Lucy says.

"Yeah," says Ben.

A few moments later, they join us in the tent.

Kit

It's the next day. We're taking a break (finally!) from driving. I *love* this marketplace! Who *knew* you could find such bargains on a Native American reservation? All these ladies have their stuff spread out on blankets, and you can just walk around and check it out. *Way* more fun than Target.

I'm trying on these funky earrings while Lucy, Ben, and Mimi look through a nearby booth. I want to ask how I look but they're talking. And it sounds serious.

"So," Mimi asks. "We'll be in Tucson tomorrow?"

Lucy nods. "Around six, I think."

Her voice sounds a little small, a little unsure.

"Are you nervous?" Ben asks her.

"A little," she admits. "Do you think I should call and tell her I'm coming? Or is it better to just show up? I should just show up, right?"

Clearly, my advice is needed. I stroll over, still modeling the earrings. "Surprise is always better," I say in my wisest voice.

Lucy just nods.

"She's gonna be real happy to see you," Mimi says.

Lucy doesn't look so sure.

Later, much later. We've passed through western Texas, all hilly. Now it's totally dark. Mimi and I are in the backseat. I'm doing her hair in tiny braids. She has the most incredible hair!

Up front, Lucy is painting her toenails with my "Flame" nail polish. I suggested something more neutral, but she insisted on red.

The car is quiet, kind of cozy.

Then Lucy breaks the silence. "Ben?" she asks.

"Yeah?"

"Were you really in jail?"

I take a sudden breath, and I feel Mimi do the same. We both lean forward, just the tiniest bit.

"Yeah," Ben tells her, "I was."

Lucy's quiet for a second. Then she asks the question we all want to ask. I can tell she's trying to sound casual. "So, you killed a guy?"

"Who said I killed a guy?" Ben sounds shocked.

Mimi leans forward. "Everybody back home," she says, like it's common knowledge.

"I didn't kill a guy," Ben says. His hands are gripping the steering wheel, and he's facing straight ahead.

"What *did* you do?" Lucy asks.

Ben doesn't answer right away. He just drives for a while. I'm holding my breath, and I think the others are, too. I'm still clutching this one braid in my hands, but I haven't moved since Lucy first spoke.

Finally, Ben starts talking. "I was at college," he says. "And I get this call from my kid sister. She wants me to come get her because my stepfather is beating her up pretty bad and my mom can't stop him. So I drive home in the middle of the night and my sister throws her stuff out the window and climbs out. And I drive her back to school in Ohio with me."

He says that all in one breath, without stopping or pausing.

When he finishes, we're all quiet for a second. Then Lucy says, "You went to jail for that?"

Ben tries to explain. "She's not really my sister. She's my stepfather's kid. And there's this law against an adult driving a child who's not a relative across state lines. My stepfather pressed charges. It wasn't too bad. I only got six months and then I had to stay in Ohio for a year's probation. But my sister got to live with her mom."

I let out a breath. I was wondering about the girl.

"What about college?" Lucy asks.

Ben gives a little shrug. "They kicked me out. I wasn't doing too good there, anyway." He pauses. "I don't know. In a way, it's terrifying because now I don't know what I'm going to do with my life. But in a way, it's, like, exhilarating."

"Why?" Lucy asks.

He looks over at her with this huge grin on his face. "Because I don't know what I'm going to do with my life."

We all nod. I think I get that. I really do.

He drives on, and we all sit there digesting what we've learned. Then, out of the darkness, Ben says, "You all really thought I killed a guy?"

"Well," says Lucy, "yeah."

Mimi and I both nod in agreement.

Ben shakes his head. "What were you *thinking*, getting in the car with a homicidal maniac?"

And we all crack up.

LUCY

Wow. This is it. Ben pulls the car to a stop in front of a big house, one story with red tiles on the roof. I think it's built out of this stuff called *adobe*, like mud bricks. It looks Spanish-y. I stare at it. "There's a car in the drive," I say, "so I guess she's home. It's — bigger than I imagined." I think of the tiny house Pop and I share.

I turn around in my seat to face Mimi and Kit. "So, you'll call and tell me everything about the audition, right?" Suddenly, I can't stand to say good-bye to them.

"You could still come with us," Mimi says. Her eyes are big and dark and glistening a little.

"Yeah," Kit says. "We're not leaving town until tomorrow."

I turn away. I can't stand to look at their pleading faces. "No," I say, "I'm sure she'll invite me to spend the night and, if she's not too busy, maybe I'll stay longer. And I know she'll get me a ticket home. I'll be fine."

I reach over the seat to hug each of them in turn. Then I get out of the car. Ben gets out, too. We meet at the back of the car, and he unloads my backpack.

I reach out for it, unable to control the shaking in my hand. "Well, I guess this is it," I say. My voice is shaky, too.

Ben looks at me, his eyes intense. "Lucy?"

"What?"

He leans forward and I feel his lips, soft and light, on my forehead. Then he steps back. "Good luck," is all he says.

I try to smile, but it isn't easy. I pick up my backpack, and, without looking back at the car, I head up the driveway. I hear the car door slam as Ben gets back in. But I don't hear the motor start.

Before I know it, I'm on the doorstep. I take a deep breath, reach out, and ring the bell.

A few moments — or is it hours? — later the door opens. My mother is standing there. She's elegant. Rich looking. There's puzzlement in her eyes. "Can I help you?" she asks.

I take a baby step forward, even though part of me wants to turn tail and run back to the car and Ben, Mimi, and Kit. "It's me, Mama," I say. "Lucy."

Her face falls. She takes a step back, holding the door open. "Come in," she says.

Except for the look on her face, it's everything I dreamed of. I turn and wave to my friends. They wave back, and Ben starts the car. Before it's even out of sight, I follow my mother inside.

With a gesture, she indicates that I should drop my backpack near the door. Then she leads me into the living room, which looks like something out of a magazine. I perch on a cream-colored couch while she moves around the room, straightening a magazine here, a vase of flowers there. She seems — nervous. Maybe even more nervous than I am. She keeps staring at me, which makes me feel really uncomfortable.

Fishing desperately for something to say, I finally come up with "You have a real nice house."

She smiles a gracious smile. "Thank you, Lucy."

It feels so totally strange to hear her say my name!

After that, we're both quiet for a while, until I try again. "Tucson seems like a nice city." Could I *be* any more lame?

"It is," she agrees. Then she smooths her skirt and looks straight at me. "Can I ask why you're here, Lucy?"

She catches me off guard. How am I supposed to answer that? All I can think to say is the truth. "I just . . . wanted to see you."

She nods, taking that in. "And why was that, Lucy?"

"Well . . ." It seems obvious to me, but I guess she needs to hear it. "You're my mother."

Now she sits down across from me. "Lucy —" she begins.

Suddenly, I can't *stand* the way she's saying my name. "Why do you keep saying my name like that?" I burst out. This isn't going the way I expected. Not at all. If I allowed myself to think about it at all, I pictured hugs and tears. Not this strained conversation, this polite chitchat.

"Like what, Lucy?" she asks, doing it again.

"Like it's some kind of disease" is what pops into my mind — and out of my mouth.

She sighs. "I'm trying very hard to be understanding of your needs," she says, sounding like some guidance-counselor pamphlet. "I guess I'm not doing a very good job." She gets to her feet again and starts pacing around. "You caught me on a bad day. I had to take off early from work because I'm having a dinner party, and —"

Just then, the phone rings. She looks up. "Hold on a moment," she says.

She walks out of the room.

To keep from crying, I look around, taking in my surroundings. That's when I notice the family pictures. They look like some family on TV — perfect and golden. The biggest one features my mother posed against a phony "clouds" backdrop in a photographer's studio, with a handsome man and two adorable little boys.

Just as I'm taking this in, she returns.

"I have brothers?" I ask. It takes an effort to push the words out.

She takes a breath. "Well, yes."

"How old are they?" I really want to know.

"Ten and seven," she says. She smiles, and I know she's thinking of her darling boys.

"Do they know about me?" I ask.

The smile droops a little. Then she pastes it back on. "Would you like some juice?" she asks.

I stand up. "No, thank you," I say very politely. "I'm — I'm going to go."

She takes a step forward. "Lucy. Wait."

I shake my head. "You're offering me juice? *Juice,* Mama?"

She comes up to me and puts a hand on my shoulder. It feels warm. Comforting. I want to relax into that touch. Then she says, "I'd like it better if you called me Caroline."

I freeze in place. Everything's frozen. My mind. My body. My heart.

"My family's important to me," she goes on. "I hope you won't want to intrude on that."

MImI

It's pouring outside. I thought it never rained in the desert! But the rain is coming down in sheets.

Inside room twenty-four at the Stetson Inn, Kit and I are practicing some dance moves for the audition while Ben plunks notes on his keyboard, jotting them down on a pad of paper as he plays.

Then there's a knock at the door.

Ben drops his pencil. Kit and I stand still. Ben jumps up, opens the door. And there's Lucy, standing there soaked to the skin, her backpack beside her. She's shaking. But she's calm. Too calm.

"Lucy." Ben pulls her into the room, and Kit and I hurry over.

"Lucy, what's wrong?" Kit asks.

"What happened?" I reach out for her.

She doesn't move. Ben takes her backpack and puts it

down on the floor very gently. "Mimi," he says, "get some towels."

I fly to the bathroom and grab every towel off the rack. When I come back, Kit is unbuttoning Lucy's sopping-wet sweater and peeling it off. Her tank top is soaked, too. Ben grabs a towel from me and wraps it around her shoulders.

"Lucy?" Ben asks.

It's eerie that she hasn't spoken yet.

Finally, she says something. "I'm fine. Really. I'm okay." But her voice sounds funny. Hollow.

"You got to see your mom, right?" I ask. When she waved good-bye, she looked happy. Like everything was going to be okay. I was glad for her, even though I knew how much we'd miss her.

"Caroline," she says. "Yes, I saw her."

"And?" Kit asks.

We know it can't be good.

Ben shakes his head at Kit, as if to say she shouldn't have asked.

But Lucy's already shrugging. Her eyes are empty. "She offered me juice." Then she walks away from us, into the bathroom. She closes the door behind her.

We look at one another. What are we supposed to do now?

Ben

Me again. I think I'm the only one who can tell this part. Lucy won't. And the others weren't there.

I knock on the bathroom door. My arms are full of dry clothes we've taken out of Lucy's backpack. There's no answer, so I try the doorknob. Surprisingly, it's not locked. I slip inside. Lucy's sitting on the floor, staring at the wall. "I thought you might want some dry clothes," I say.

"Thanks." Her voice is flat.

I start to leave, thinking she just wants to be alone. Then, something makes me turn back. I sit down on the floor next to her.

"I'm fine," she says, even though I didn't ask.

"I know you are," I say, even though I know she's not.

"I really am."

"I know."

There's silence between us. I reach out and take her

hand. She leans toward me and puts her head against my chest. I hug her tight. I can feel her wet tears on my shirt.

We sit that way for a few minutes. I just stroke her hair quietly. Finally, I have to ask. "What happened?"

Lucy takes a long breath. There's a little sob in it. "She didn't want me. She never wanted me. She said my father made her have me. She said it was a mistake."

Then she starts to cry. Really cry. I can see how much it hurts. I put my arms around her and pull her close.

Kit

The rain finally slows down. Then it stops. Lucy and Mimi and I go out and sit by the pool in the dark, watching the water reflect the lights of the motel. We sit close to one another. Mimi and I are kind of stroking Lucy's hair, trying to comfort her. She's stopped crying, and she's very, very quiet.

"I look like her, you know?" she tells us. "I have her eyes. And her hands."

"You got the best parts," Mimi says, holding one of Lucy's hands.

"It's her loss, Lucy," I say.

My words sound empty. Lucy looks down at the water. "It's weird. I don't have a mother."

Mimi leans in and presses her cheek against Lucy's. "You have us," she says.

"Yeah," I say, wrapping my arms around her.

*　*　*

The next morning, the sun is shining as if it had never rained. I'm on the phone. Suddenly, I need to hear Dylan's voice. But he's not there. "Well, can you tell him I called?" I ask the guy who answered. "Thanks." I hang up. Lucy's just coming out of the bathroom, brushing her hair. Mimi is dressing over on the other side of the room. She was pretending not to listen, but I know she heard.

"He wasn't there?" Lucy asks.

It's truth time. These girls need to know the real deal. I swallow hard. "Dylan didn't invite me," I tell them, looking down at my hands. "He doesn't know I'm coming. Lately he's been . . . I mean, I'm sure everything's fine between us. Really. But he didn't invite me."

"Oh, Kit." Lucy comes over to put her arms around me.

"Do you think the girls in L.A. are prettier than me?" I ask. I'm so pathetic sometimes.

"Shut up," Mimi says. "You're beautiful."

"I'm just being stupid," I say, trying to smile.

Lucy decides to change the subject. "Where's Ben?" she asks.

I give her a grateful look. "I think he went to fill up the car."

"We're gonna get some breakfast," Mimi tells Lucy. "Wanna come?"

It's so great to have Lucy back with us. I mean, I'm sorry about the reason, but the girl belongs with us, right?

But she shakes her head. "No. I need to call my father. Get him to send me a ticket."

"Luce, don't go home," Mimi pleads. "You should come to L.A. with us."

"Yeah," I agree.

"If you come, we could all audition together. It'd be like singing in the car," Mimi tells her.

"I don't know. My father —"

Mimi won't give up. "If you sing lead, we could win."

The girl is right. "It'll be fun," I say. "Please?"

"Please?" Mimi echoes. "It'll be so much fun."

We both look at her, begging with our eyes. But she just shakes her head. "I can't," she says.

LUCy

I know Mimi and Kit are disappointed. They probably have no idea how disappointed I am. I would love to come with them. I really would. But I know what I have to do.

I'm sitting on the bed in our hotel room with the phone on my lap. I pick it up and dial — then hang up, before the call can go through. This is so hard. I pick up the phone again, dial again . . . and hang up again. I stare at the wall, thinking.

"Trying to call your father?"

I look up to see Ben leaning against the door frame, watching me.

I nod. "I can't seem to — but I will in a minute." I feel so empty. Even seeing Ben doesn't cheer me up.

"Can I see that poem you read me, back in the desert?" he asks.

I'm a little surprised. "Sure," I say. What's the difference? I dig my journal out of my backpack, find the right page, and hand it to him. "Why?"

He ducks his head. "I made you something."

"What?"

"It's a surprise." He grabs my hand and pulls me off the bed. "Come and see."

He leads me down hallways and through doors; it's like a guided tour of the whole motor lodge. I still don't get what's going on. Then he opens a final door and goes inside. I follow him.

It's a huge, empty room that the Stetson Inn uses for banquets and weddings and things. Ugly carpeting, horrendous lighting, cheap-looking tables and chairs. In one corner, there's a baby grand piano.

Ben sees my face. "It's ugly, isn't it?" he asks.

"Yeah. Is this my surprise?" I'm disappointed, but trying not to let it show.

He laughs. "Wouldn't it be so sad if it was? Like, if I was this bad at cheering people up?"

I laugh, too. Ben is so — Ben.

He reaches into his pocket and comes up with a piece of paper. When he hands it to me, I see that it's music paper with notes written out. "I wrote some music," he says. "For your poem."

Wow. "You did?" Nobody ever did anything like that for me before.

"Yes" is all Ben says.

"Will you play it for me?" I stare down at the notes.

"Will you sing?" he asks.

Our eyes meet. I nod. "Okay."

Ben takes my hand and leads me over to the piano. Gently, he picks me up and sits me down on it. He smiles at me. He seems shy all of a sudden. A little nervous. A little embarrassed. Looking at him, I feel my heart swell.

He points to a section of the music. "Just use this for the refrain, okay?"

"Okay." I still can't believe this is happening.

Ben starts to play. The melody is so beautiful I almost forget to sing, but he nods at me and I come in right on time, singing my very own words.

This has to be the most romantic moment of my life.

I want the song to last forever, but all too soon Ben is playing the final chords. When we finish, there's complete silence in the room. I feel so connected to him; it's like we're one person, just for that moment.

He looks up at me. "Do you like it?"

I slide off the piano and sit next to him on the bench. "I can't believe you went to all the trouble to make my poem a song," I tell him. It's not what I *want* to say, but it's all I can think of right that second.

He just looks at me. "It was no trouble at all," he says. He leans toward me.

I lean toward him.

Centuries pass.

And then. And then we kiss.

His lips are so soft. I'm melting.

We pull away from each other. I can't look at him. Then I do, and he's looking straight at me.

We smile.

Hours later, I stand at the pay phone outside the Stetson Inn's office while Ben loads luggage into the car. Mimi and Kit are watching me. Their faces are tense.

I dial. Listen to the ring on the other end. Then Pop's voice comes on. "Hi, you've reached Pete and Lucy," he says. "Leave a message." There's a long beep.

I don't have to identify myself. He knows my voice. I start talking. "I'm just calling to say that . . ." I glance over at Mimi and Kit. At Ben. ". . . that I'm fine. And Pop? You were right. About Mama. You were right." It's not easy to control my voice. I hang up. Then I walk over to the car and toss my backpack into the open trunk.

"I'm going to L.A. with you," I tell them.

mimi

I couldn't be happier. I mean, what could be better than driving through California (yes, we're finally there!) in a convertible with your two best friends?

We girls are all in the backseat, laughing and talking happily. I still can hardly believe that Lucy is with us. I am so psyched. We watch the desert whiz by. The sun warms our shoulders. Life is good.

Then Ben reaches forward and turns on the radio. Uh-oh. Metal time. But, no! He finds a pop station and turns it up, way up. I glance in the mirror, trying to meet his eyes. He looks back, like, "What?" I grin at him and start singing along. Then he starts singing, too!

"Whooo!" I cry as Ben turns onto the highway. There it is. The Pacific Ocean! It's blue, and clear, and everything I always dreamed it would be. It's absolutely gorgeous.

LUCy

We find the perfect motel, right on the edge of the beach. The ocean stretches out forever, all blue and beautiful. I can't believe we're really here!

Mimi and Kit and I head straight for the water and plunge in. I feel everything wash away as we dive through the surf, laughing and screaming with joy.

This just feels right.

After a few minutes, I walk out of the surf and join Ben on the beach, where he's been sitting on the sand, watching us.

I pick up a shell and toss it at him. "I can't believe we're finally here."

"I know," he says. He reaches out and runs his warm hands over my back.

My head is full of thoughts. "Ben, you know," I say, "there are plenty of colleges in L.A."

He's quiet for a second. "Yeah."

"So . . . what if I didn't go back?" I've barely allowed myself to even think this. I can't believe I'm saying it out loud.

"Lucy . . ." Ben looks at me. His face is very serious.

"Why shouldn't I do what I want for once?" I think of the job Pop lined up for me. Medical school. All of it. I shake my head. "And I want to stay," I say. "I'm going to stay." I look out over the ocean. Something about this place feels like home. I turn to face Ben, wondering what he'll say.

"You gotta do what you gotta do," he says.

"No," I say. "You don't."

We smile at each other, and he reaches out to wrap me in his arms. I lean against him, and we gaze out at Mimi and Kit frolicking in the surf. They're splashing each other, acting like little kids. I see Mimi stop for a second and look down at her beautiful, huge belly, patting it lovingly. "Look how happy she is," I say, watching her. I don't think I've seen her smile like that since we were both eight years old.

MIMI

I look up at the sign. I still can't believe it. I've been thinking about this moment for months, and now it's finally here. I read the sign to myself: SLIDE RECORDS OPEN AUDITION SIGN-UP. It's finally time.

I don't care how long the line is. All I care about is that I'm standing in it. Me, Mimi. And my friends are with me.

One of the organizers finally gets to us. He hands me a form. He looks bored, like he doesn't care. "Fill this out," he says in a monotone, "and turn it in over there." He nods over his shoulder at a desk. "The audition is in six days."

Mimi and Kit lean over my shoulder to see the form. Lucy rummages in her backpack and finds a pen. She gives it to me so I can fill out the form. I glance at all the blank spaces. My heart sinks a little. "What are we gonna do about music?" I ask.

Ben is reassuring. "I'll put up some fliers," he promises, "try to get a band together for you guys. I know a few people out here."

I like that.

I look at the form again and start filling it in.

Kit

"Dylan?" Finally! I got him on the phone. I'm so excited. He's gonna flip when he hears where I am!

"Guess where I am?" I ask. "L.A.!"

I look over at Ben, Lucy, and Mimi. They're with me in the motel room, unpacking. I try not to let my face show my disappointment. Dylan is not exactly flipping.

"Well, then, I'll come to you," I say, trying to keep my voice bright and cheerful. "How about tonight?" I glance at Lucy again. She's listening, I can tell. "Okay, then, tomorrow morning?"

I can't believe he's putting me off. Doesn't he want to see me? His fiancée? Now Mimi's looking at me, too. So's Ben. Ben looks sort of sad. "Dylan," I say, lowering my voice a little and turning away from the two of them, "I'm in Los Angeles. I came here to see you." I listen. His words make no sense. But I just nod. "Fine . . . I said, fine."

I hang up. Then I look around at my friends. I paste a smile on my face, the one I use for pictures. "He's really busy," I explain. They nod. They understand. I mean, after all, everybody's busy, right? Who can't relate to *that*? I jump to my feet. "Who wants to go sight-seeing?"

Mimi's the only one who raises her hand.

"Lucy?" I ask. "Ben?"

I see the two of them look at each other. "I'm really . . ." Lucy says, ". . . tired. I'm really tired."

"Yeah," says Ben. He sure is a man of few words.

But we *need* Ben. "We can't go anywhere without a car to drive," I say.

Ben reaches into his pocket and tosses me the keys. Automatically, I reach out to catch them. "Don't crash," he says.

That's all? He hands over his precious car and that's all he says?

"All right!" Mimi pumps a fist in the air.

"Still," I say, wishing they'd come along, "it would be more fun if we all went. . . ."

Mimi grabs my arm. "Can't you take a hint?" she asks.

Oh. Duh. I look at Lucy, who's looking at Ben. I get it. I let Mimi drag me out of the room.

We jump in the car and head out with the top down. We're in L.A.! I drive with one hand, checking the map I'm holding in the other. I make a left, a right, another left.

Mimi looks confused. "I thought we were going to see the Hollywood sign," she says.

"We will," I promise.

"But," she says, sounding bewildered, "it's that way." She points in the opposite direction.

"We're making a stop first," I tell her. I check the map again and take a right down a one-way street. Then I sneak a peek over at Mimi. She's figured it out.

"Kit, you can see Dylan tomorrow," she says.

"No," I say, feeling strangely calm and in control. "I want to see him now." I turn the wheel hard, and the car screeches around a corner.

A few minutes later, I pull up in front of an apartment building. It looks just like all the other buildings around here. But it's special. I know this address by heart, from all the letters I've sent here. This is where Dylan lives.

Mimi doesn't want to come with me, but I beg her. She follows me up the long flight of stairs to his door. When we get there, I raise my hand to knock, but she turns around.

"I really should wait in the car," she says.

"Mimi, no!" I need her with me. "How do I look?" I ask.

"You look great," she answers, without even looking at me. "But Kit, I'm sure you'll want to be alone together and —" She starts to move away again, but I grab her arm.

She just sighs. I knock on the door. After a moment, it swings open.

Dylan looks cuter than ever. I forgot how tall he is, how strong. How dark his eyes are. He stares at me. He's holding a beer in one hand, a cigarette in the other.

"Surprise," I say.

He *is* surprised, I can tell. But it's not, like, a *happy* kind of surprised. Still, he leans over and kisses me. "Kitty Cat," he says. "I thought we were going to make plans tomorrow." Then his eyes go to Mimi. He blinks a little, like he's not sure what he's seeing.

"This is my friend —" I begin.

"Mimi," Dylan finishes. "Hey."

"Hey," says Mimi.

I'm confused. I look at Dylan, then at Mimi. "You know each other?"

Dylan grins. That slow, sexy grin of his that always drove me crazy. "From school," he says. "Right, Mimi?"

Something weird is going on here. I can feel it.

"Right," Mimi agrees. Why does she sound — angry?

"Oh. Well," I say. "Aren't you going to invite us in?" I try to see around Dylan's shoulders. How many times have I tried to imagine what this place looks like?

He doesn't budge. "I would, Kitty Cat, but — I've got a friend here. He's really upset and we were supposed to, you know, hang out."

He's lying. He never was a good liar. But why would he lie? "Oh," I say. What else *can* I say?

"I'm really sorry," he says, all smooth. "Why don't you come over tomorrow morning? Bring your bags and you can stay with me."

That sounds better. Maybe I misjudged him. Maybe everything's going to be fine, after all. "Okay," I say. "I'll see you tomorrow."

"I love you," he says.

Oh, Dylan. "I love you, too," I say, leaning forward to kiss him. "Bye, sweetie," I murmur into his ear.

Just then, I hear a woman's voice from inside the apartment. "Do you need money for the pizza?"

I freeze. Step back. Glare at him. "Your friend is really upset?" I *knew* the man was lying.

"Kitty Cat —" He reaches out for me, but I push past him and stalk into his living room. There's this chick there, sitting on the sofa. She's, like, totally L.A. Totally gorgeous. Wearing one of his shirts.

She looks me over. "Who's she?"

She means me. She wants to know who I am? I'll tell her. "We're supposed to be getting married," I say to Dylan. "We're supposed to be getting married," I repeat, turning back to Miss L.A.

She gets up and leaves the room.

I look at Dylan. "I was going to tell you," he says, holding up his hands, "but I just didn't want to do it over the phone."

I feel tears coming to my eyes. No! I don't want to cry! I *won't* cry! "But . . . but you gave me a ring. You proposed, and you gave me a ring."

"Kitty . . ." He raises his beer to his lips and takes a sip. It's one of those fancy imported beers. The one in a blue bottle.

Suddenly, I *know.*

I turn around, very slowly. I look at Mimi. "It was Dylan, wasn't it?" I ask.

She won't meet my eyes. "I . . . I . . ." She can't answer.

"He was the guy at Christmas," I go on. I see it in her eyes. I'm right. I turn back to Dylan. "It was you, wasn't it?"

He looks frightened, then angry. "What are you talking about?"

Suddenly, it all comes together. "I knew there was something. You came over that night. You were acting strange. It was the same night, wasn't it?"

"Kitty, what's your problem?"

I narrow my eyes and stare him down. "The whole time, the whole trip, I knew it was you. I did. I just couldn't admit it." It's true. I feel horrible, like I wish the earth would swallow me up. How could I have been so nasty to Mimi, when it was Dylan I was angry at the whole time?

"I have to get out of here," Mimi says just then. Her voice is shaking.

"Wait." I reach out to stop her. "I want him to admit it." I keep staring at Dylan.

"You're getting yourself all worked up over nothing, Kitty Cat," he says, as if he's talking to a little kid.

I let my lower lip tremble a little bit. I turn away. Then I ball up my fist, carefully keeping my thumb on the outside, and I hit Dylan hard, right under his chin. He goes down. I look at him, shaking my head. "You jerk," I say. "My name's not Kitty Cat. I'm not your pet." I want to say more, but just then Mimi breaks away and runs for the stairs. "Mimi!" I yell. "Mimi, wait!"

She's almost all the way down the stairs when it happens. Her foot catches on a step. For a second, I think she'll catch herself, but she doesn't.

I'll never forget watching her fall.

Her little globe key ring goes flying through the air.

LUCy

I'm sleeping when the call comes. Mimi's at the hospital.

Soon we're *all* at the hospital. Ben and Kit and I slump in the waiting room. Ben's leaning against a window, and Kit's head is in my lap. We all look up when the doctor comes over.

It's not good news.

After the doctor leaves, I go to the pay phone and make a call.

A day later, we're still at the hospital. I wait outside. Finally, a cab pulls up and Pop gets out. He comes over and hugs me. Hard. I look over his shoulder, and I see a new mother getting wheeled out by her husband. She looks happy. Her little baby is all wrapped up cozy, with just its little pink face showing.

I hold Pop closer and a sob breaks loose.

mImi

I'm ready to get out of this place. I can't stand the room. I can't stand the gown. I can't stand the stupid bracelet with my name on it. I'm tugging at it when Lucy walks into my room. She comes over to stand by my bed.

"They said I lost the baby," I say. "Lost it. Like I put it down somewhere and now I can't find it." My voice is flat. I look down at the bracelet. "Like it was my keys or something. Isn't that the stupidest thing you ever heard?" I look up at Lucy. "Did you call my mother?" I know I sound mad. I *am* mad, but not at Lucy. I hope she knows that.

"Yeah," Lucy says. "But . . ."

Ha. No surprise. "She's not coming," I say. "Yeah. I didn't think she would." I can't stand the sympathy in Lucy's eyes. "So, neither of us have mothers," I say. "And now *I'm* not a mother."

She sits down on the bed next to me, but she doesn't touch me or anything.

"I'd decided to keep it, you know," I tell her. "Her." The baby was a girl. That's what the doctor said. A little girl. "I was standing on the beach and my toes were in the Pacific Ocean and she kicked. And it was like this sign. So I decided to keep her."

Now Lucy reaches out to stroke my leg.

I push her hand away. "Don't touch me. I'm not ready to cry."

Lucy takes her hand back. "Okay."

I lean back against my pillows. I'm going to cry, anyway. "I would have made such a good mom."

LUCY

Pop is furious. He's not yelling because there are too many people around, but I can tell it's a struggle for him to keep his voice down.

We're standing outside Mimi's room, and he's leaning over me. "What were you thinking, huh? Running away. And with a pregnant girl. What were you thinking?" He looks at me. I don't have anything to say. "Lucy! I'm waiting for an answer."

People turn to stare as they walk by. Pop notices, and he backs away a little, calms himself.

"She wanted to see the ocean," I say finally.

"What?"

"Nothing." There's no way he'll ever understand.

"I had to close down the shop to come here. Take money out of the savings for plane fare, hotel. . . . You *know* how hard I worked to save that money for your college."

What can I say? "I'm sorry" seems to be the only thing I can manage.

He sighs. He looks really tired. "All right. You made a mistake. I understand. We all make mistakes. You're forgiven." He tries to smile at me. "I'm going to get you girls back home where you belong, and we'll forget all about this. Okay?"

I just nod.

"Who was that boy you were with?" he asks suddenly. "How old is he? Was he the one who talked you girls into this crazy idea?"

Ben. "No," I say. "He's . . . he just gave us a ride."

Later, I'm in our hotel room, packing, when a piece of paper falls out of my backpack. I pick it up. It's the music that Ben wrote for my poem. I sit down on the bed, holding it. Staring at it. I trace the notes with my fingers.

Ben

She's so beautiful, sitting there. I come into our motel room to find Lucy sitting on the bed, looking down at a piece of paper. When I go over to her, she jumps up. She looks surprised to see me.

I kiss her.

I'm still not used to that, that I can kiss her anytime I want.

I can't wait to tell her my news. "My uncle thinks he might know of an apartment I can rent. You and I are supposed to go see it tomorrow," I tell her, holding her hand. Then I look around. And I realize what she's doing.

She's packing.

"What are you doing?" I ask, even though I just figured it out.

"Packing," she says. "My father says I have to move to his hotel."

"Until the audition?" I ask. "How are we going to rehearse?" This is going to mess up everything.

"I'm not going to the audition," Lucy says. She won't look at me.

"Lucy?" I ask. I can't believe what I'm hearing. What is she *talking* about? Of course she has to go to the audition.

"I have to go back with him," she tells me. She still won't meet my eyes.

Him. She means her father. I know I should understand, but I just don't. "Oh."

She moves closer to me. "Ben," she says, pleading. "He's my father. And I can't just —"

I take a step back. I can't stand it. "I get it," I say. And I walk out of the room.

Kit

I stand outside the door to Mimi's hospital room, gripping this stupid bouquet of flowers I bought at the gift shop. What was I thinking? I mean, *flowers*?

I stare at the door, count to three. On "three," I'll knock.
One.
Two.
Three.
I can't do it! She must hate me.

I take a deep breath. Then I knock gently on the door. I push it open and see Mimi sitting in a chair next to her bed. I look at her, waiting for her to turn away.

"Did you see how fast he went down?" she asks. "That's because you threw your whole body into the punch, just like I taught you. You did really good."

That's when I start to cry.

*   *   *

That night, we take Mimi home from the hospital. Well, not *home* exactly. We take her to the Sunset Star Motel. And we pack.

Lucy's dad is taking us all home.

We're sitting in the lobby the next day, luggage at our feet, waiting for Lucy's dad to check us out of the motel. I don't think I'm the only one holding back tears. Nothing worked out. We came all the way to L.A., and nothing worked out. I'm tired. "I can't believe we're going home already," I say finally, just to break the silence.

"I know," Lucy agrees.

"Dylan called," I tell them, "to ask for his ring back." I know *that'll* get a reaction.

Mimi makes a face. "He doesn't deserve his ring back."

"That's what I told him." I hold up my hand, where the ring still shines on my finger. Then I pull it off. Oh, well. "You can't be pretty forever, right?"

Mimi looks at me, then at Lucy. She clears her throat. "I just wanna say . . . thanks."

"For what?" Lucy asks.

"For coming on this trip with me," she answers simply.

How can she be so sweet, when everything was such a disaster?

"I'm sorry about the audition, Mimi," says Lucy.

Mimi just shrugs. "Who needs it? I could go to college instead. I mean, so what if I'm from a trailer park?" Then she's quiet for a second. "Besides," she continues, "I didn't want you two to come on this trip for the audition."

Lucy looks surprised. "What *did* you want?"

I answer for her. "She wanted you. And me. She wanted us."

Mimi looks at me gratefully and nods. "I just wanted my friends back."

We hold the look for a second. Then I turn to Lucy. "Mimi and I have been talking," I tell her. "And we think . . ."

"We think you should stay and go to the audition," Mimi finishes my sentence.

"Guys . . ." Lucy looks upset.

"You have to go, Luce. For us." Of all of us, Lucy's the one who could really be a star.

"We have big dreams for you," Mimi adds.

Lucy just sits there, lost in thought, until her dad comes over. "You ready to go?" he asks.

We look at her. Maybe — maybe she really will change her mind!

But she just nods at him.

"Yeah," she says.

And the bellman picks up our bags, and we follow him outside.

Lucy

I know they're disappointed. But they can't be more disappointed than I am. I'm watching the bellman load our stuff into the trunk of a taxi when Ben calls me. "Lucy!" I turn to see him standing under the hotel's awning. I look at Pop next to me. Then I walk over to Ben.

"You came," I say.

"Yeah."

I want to say more, but I can't.

"Good-bye, Lucy," he says.

"Good-bye."

And then I can't stand it another second. I step forward and throw my arms around him, as if I could hold him forever.

"Lucy?" Pop calls.

I pull away from Ben and walk like a robot to the cab.

I look back at Ben as I climb in with the others. The bell-man shuts the door. And the cab pulls away.

Kit's up front. Mimi, Pop, and I are in the backseat, with Pop in the middle. He takes my hand. "It's gonna be good to get back home, right?"

I can't answer. I just watch out the window as the cab moves away and Ben grows smaller and smaller.

Pop keeps talking. "Listen. I'm sorry if I yelled at you before. I was angry at what you did, not at you. Okay?" This time he doesn't expect an answer. He just kisses me on the forehead and sits back in his seat.

Kit's looking at me from the front seat. I feel Mimi's eyes on me, too. I can practically hear what they're thinking. *Say something!* Their voices ring inside my head. *Say it now!*

The cab is still moving. I put my hand on the locket that hangs around my neck. "Pop."

He looks at me.

I take the locket off and hold it out to him. He won't take it. I manage to speak. "I don't want to be like her," I say.

Like my mother. Like Caroline. She wanted something else. And to find it, she had to leave us.

He knows what I'm talking about. "Lucy," he says soothingly, "we'll get home and everything will go back to normal. Just wait and —"

I won't let him finish. I press the locket into his hand. "Don't make me do what she did."

He opens the locket and stares down at the picture. The picture of me and my mother. His wife. Then he looks up at me, and I see the fear in his eyes. "Don't make me run," I beg him. "Let me go."

Ben

I'm watching the cab disappear, feeling as if my heart were just torn out of my chest, when I realize that it has stopped.

Then the door flies open and Lucy jumps out. She runs back up the hotel driveway. Behind her, Mimi and Kit climb out of the cab, too. And Lucy's dad. He gets out slowly and stands there, watching her.

Watching her run straight into my arms.

Audition night.

I'm watching Lucy, all alone up there on the stage. She looks more beautiful than ever. And she's singing her heart out.

I watch from the wings. I can see the judges in the audience. They look hypnotized, leaning forward in their seats.

Mimi and Kit are onstage, too, singing backup. They look relaxed and confident.

In the middle of the song, Lucy looks over at me. I'm in the wings, playing keyboard with the band I put together. I give her a wink.

She's amazing.

Incredible.

Even better than that night in New Orleans.

The judges are starting to look excited, and the crowd is loving it.

By the time she finishes, the audience is all hers. Especially her dad. He's standing there, yelling louder than anyone else and clapping his hands over his head. Even from here, I can see that there are tears in his eyes.

And Lucy? She stands there onstage, soaking it in. She looks so happy. So — *herself.*

Epilogue: Lucy

This time, we're old enough to realize that we have *no* idea where life's going to take us.

We dig a deep hole in the sand. The moon shines bright overhead, and the lights of Santa Monica glow in the distance.

The plastic box sits, waiting to be buried. This one isn't covered with glitter. And it won't hold our dreams for the future. We don't know where we'll end up, but we do know where we've been.

Kit, gorgeous, tosses in her sparkling engagement ring.

Mimi adds her hospital bracelet.

Carefully, I place my journal in the middle.

Then I add one more thing. A picture.

It's the three of us dancing around in that hotel room in New Orleans. Happy.

The only thing certain about our future is this: Ten years from now, when it's time to open this box, we'll still be friends.